SKY DADDY

CANAAN PARKER

alyson
books

LOS ANGELES • NEW YORK

Manufactured in the United States of America.
Printed on acid-free paper.

This trade paperback original is published by Alyson Publications Inc.,
P.O. Box 4371, Los Angeles, California 90078-4371.
Distribution in the United Kingdom by Turnaround Publisher Services Ltd.,
Unit 3 Olympia Trading Estate, Coburg Road, Wood Green,
London N22 6TZ, England.

First edition: October 1997

01 00 99 98 97   10 9 8 7 6 5 4 3 2 1

ISBN 1-55583-398-5

Library of Congress Cataloging-in-Publication Data
　　Parker, Canaan.
　　　Sky daddy / Canaan Parker. — 1st ed.
　　　ISBN 1-55583-398-5
　　　I. Title.
　　PS3566.A6749S58 1997
　　813'.54—dc21　　　　　　　　　　　97-28213 CIP

Cover design by C. Harrity.
Cover photographs by Bel Ami and Johnathan Black.

To Jenod Woodley

PRISM

Derrick goes by the nickname "Chill." As in "chill out." Or "Chiller," as in *Chiller Theater. 'Cause I'm the coolest, and I strike terror into chumps.* He is so straight. He thinks about women all the time. His father is a homosexual. A natural, delighted queer, deep violet on the spectrum of lust. Uh-oh! For most of Chill's young life, of course, he wouldn't have known what a homosexual was.

Hazily, but with a bit of sting, he still remembers the day he left his father. From the age of six to eight, he had lived happily with his dad in the Marcus Garvey Houses in Brooklyn. The morning he was to return to his mother's custody, Derrick woke to shouting and glass breaking outside his window. Fumbling with the window shade, he peered out into the grayish, just-breaking dawn. Three boys were having an argument in the grass lot below: a Puerto Rican boy with no pants on, a tall black boy, and another Puerto Rican. The pantless boy bluffed with his fists, but the others shoved him down in the dirt. The tall boy undid his belt and climbed on

3

his back as the other knelt close, smacking his face and whispering in his ear.

Then the tall boy started wiggling in the grass. Violent, bothersome undulations. Derrick looked away but then back again at the disturbing motion of hips and bare bottom. He felt sorry for the boy underneath. *He'll scrape his skin on the gravel,* he thought. The lot was littered with pebbles and glass, used firecrackers and dead insects, and he had often skinned his own flesh playing there.

After a short while, the bouncing stopped. The boys stood and argued some more. The one boy pulled on a pair of shorts; then all three ran together out of sight. Derrick went back to bed, but he couldn't fall asleep. Kicking away his sheets, he felt vaguely annoyed. Two boys with their pants down — what was it about? There was such a thing as sex, he knew about that. He had laughed about it behind the softball fence at school. But sex happened only between women and men.

Didn't it?

Later that morning Derrick was on a plane to Cincinnati with his mother and all his things. On the flight, in his imagination, he quietly relived the details of that morning. The young, hot voices; that slapping sound. The gray black boy, his undulating hips, and the gray Puerto Rican in the gray dawn, lying in the dirt as still as slain prey. His father hugging him after breakfast and saying good-bye.

Eighteen now, Derrick is flying to New York to visit his father for the summer. He slumps in his seat, his shoes off, his body curled toward the window. Radiant light bounces off the clouds, tripping along the lashes of his half-closed eyes. He wants to sleep, but he can't.

The jet passes over a great lake. The white clouds part, and Derrick can see sunlight on the water and great green squares of land in the distance. The jet trembles, tilts sharply, then flattens out, and he sees nothing again but radiant blue, white, and radiant light. He shoves himself back in his seat and becomes abruptly glum.

Damn, man. Life is too much of a trip, he thinks. *Moms is bugging. Maybe I can move in with Pop.*

The flight attendant, a young Asian woman, walks past him again toward the pilot's cabin. They had shared a laugh before when he asked her for a dry martini. "You don't look twenty-one to me," she answered, smiling warmly.

"But I have this fear of flying, sweetness. A little vodka might calm my nerves." He glances at her legs, appreciates her fine butt. He wishes again that he would fall asleep.

Old funky Pop, he thinks. *All filled up with secrets.*

He wonders about his father's private life. Especially if he does move in with him. Does Pop smoke grass? Is he dating any women? Does he keep girlie mags in a hiding place?

Derrick rests his face against the jet's glass window. He thinks of his girlfriend, Wanda, back in Cincinnati and the love they had made the night before, her crying and tenderness, knowing Derrick would be gone all summer.

The stewardess comes by and offers him a magazine.

"Can't I get *Playboy*?"

"No, you naughty person."

Derrick smiles as she walks away.

In a short while he can sleep.

Joseph Grant could barely make out what his boyfriend was saying out in the bedroom. He was in the bathroom, pulling on his pants and wondering where he had left his wallet. He had to meet his son at the airport in an hour. He stepped out of the bathroom, huffed in disbelief, and set his fists impatiently on his hips. The nineteen-year-old was still sprawled out like a duckling in the bed under a pile of pillows and sheets.

"Caleb, what are you doing? You have to split."

"How come?"

"I have to go to the airport."

"Why can't he take a taxi? He's not a little kid. Christ, he's as old as me."

Joseph sifted through the bedsheets for his wallet. Grinning, the teen stuck out his leg, blocking Joseph's hand with a bare heel.

"What are you yapping about?" asked Joseph.

The teen kicked back the sheets to reveal himself in white cotton underpants. He pushed his pelvis up on the mattress and spread his legs in an awkwardly inviting yawn. Touching himself, he looked up expectantly, but Joseph didn't see — he was hurriedly pulling a sport shirt over his head.

"Have you seen my wallet?" Joseph asked, his voice muffled in folds of blue cotton.

"Mmph mmm-umma umm."

6

"I said where is my wallet?" Joseph repeated, straightening his collar and waistline. "And get dressed, damn it. I have to leave in" — he glanced at the clock radio — "two minutes!"

"Your wallet is on the floor in the bathroom. By the shower."

"I was just in there." Joseph stepped back into the bathroom and found his wallet in a pile of towels on the floor. He counted his cash quickly. *Enough,* he thought.

When he came out of the bathroom, Caleb was standing on the bed with the white sheet over his head, teetering from side to side like a ghost. "Jo-eeey. I'm coming to take you to hell, Joey."

"Goddamn it." Joseph yanked away the sheet, only to reveal the boy completely naked, his underpants around his ankles. A burst of joy spread behind his face as he remembered, *This was why.* "Come on. I'm in a hurry."

Caleb scratched his yellow pubic hair and wiggled his hips like a showgirl. He jiggled his nuts in the palm of his hand, then started bouncing up and down on the mattress, jolting the springs, his penis flopping against his stomach.

"I don't believe this," exclaimed Joseph.

Caleb collapsed on the mattress and pulled the sheet between his legs, covering just his genitals. Joseph climbed onto the bed, found a pair of underpants, and rubbed the white cotton bikini into the teen's surprised face.

"Put…this…on," he said.

A pair of blue jeans were on the floor. A tie-dyed T-shirt was on the easy chair. "Put *these* on. Put *this* on."

"Hell!" said Caleb. "I want to have sex."

"You had enough sex. Now get dressed or I'll kick you out in the street looking like that."

Caleb let out a laugh that disintegrated into an uncertain warble. "Yeah, my dad would love it if I showed up on the porch wearing just a sheet."

"I promise we'll have sex next month."

"Next month? Oh, no, Joe," said Caleb, screwing up his face. "It's summertime. How can I survive without a man in my life?"

"It's not cool, Cal. Not while my son is in town."

Caleb sucked his teeth, stood up on the mattress again, and pulled on his jeans. Muttering curses, he plopped back down on the edge of the bed and pulled on his shoes. "You're too old, Joe. I'm getting me a hot young stud for a lover. No more Grandpa Moses *re*-jects from the Old Ladies Bridge Club."

Standing up, he tucked his Jockey shorts into his back pocket and headed toward the door. Joseph followed and stopped him just before he left the bedroom, giving him a hug and a long, warm kiss. The boy felt brittle, filled with warm blood, sparrowlike, in his arms. "I'm sorry, Cal. We'll figure it out, okay? I'll call you at work."

Caleb nodded, shook his hand politely, and walked out the door. Joseph listened until he heard the front door slam. Then he went to the window and opened it to air out the bedroom. He paused for a moment to look at the sky, which had suddenly grown cloudy.

On the stoop downstairs Caleb stopped to light a cigarette. Two boys in the fashion — baggy jeans and baseball hats —

walked by joking and dancing. Caleb smiled. *Hot numbers,* he thought.

Someone had let go of a red balloon, and he watched it float up into the hazy sky. Iron-colored clouds were moving in from the north. It was a slow-burning July Monday and felt as though a storm might blow up shortly.

I hope Joe's son lands safely, he thought. Scratching his oily hair, he wondered whether he honestly meant that. "My stepson," he murmured and laughed. "I should give him a spanking. And Joe too."

He was angry at Joe for kicking him out, even though they had spent the whole weekend together. Their last for a while, Joe kept reminding him, so they had to make it special. The old cat had tried his best. Cracking jokes, which didn't come easily for Joe, and singing him songs. And cooking, though Joey wasn't much of a cook. Cheese dogs and fried potatoes. Toaster waffles. Caleb had made a playful mess of the sunny-side-up eggs Joe had prepared for Sunday breakfast.

He did that all the time with Joey. Acted dopey. That was his privilege in this love affair. It was so conspicuous, after all. He was the little one, and Joey was the dad. Not *his* dad but *the* dad. A fine difference but one that stoked his lust for this older Negro with the rough feet, short neat hair, and youngish smile. Last night in the shower, Caleb had dug his knees into Joe's big warm hips, climbing his tall lover like a tree in a fearful passion. Taking a long drag, he quelled an urge to run back upstairs.

If Caleb was the little one, then who was Derrick? *My little brother?* he considered.

9

He pulled a crumpled twenty-dollar bill out of his pocket. He had taken it from Joseph's wallet in the bathroom. Maybe he would score a nickel bag. No, he didn't feel like getting stoned. Maybe he would go see a movie or take a long taxi ride around Central Park.

He stole money from his own dad. Pocket change first, when he was ten, then girlie magazines to sell for quarters and, if he was lucky, a pat on his butt to balding, blue-cheeked Teamsters down at the Court Street Social Club. Dollar bills as he got older. Once he took a hundred dollars plus the credit card, the weekend he ran away after his father slapped him for skipping school. His guidance counselor at school suggested he stole as an act of possessing his father. Perhaps it was so with Joseph as well. "What's yours is mine because I *am* you, so you are mine." This was Caleb's singular and very private definition of being in love.

He shrugged his shoulders and looked up as if expecting Derrick's plane to appear in the sky. He bit his lip and looked up the street. Fatherhood wasn't so sacred an emotion. His own father didn't give a fuck about him. *I'm more important to Joe,* he thought, then swept away the thought and covered it up with shame.

Footsteps were coming down the stairway behind him. Quickly Caleb stuffed the money into his pocket. Joseph came through the glass front door, jumpy and eager, stopping suddenly when he saw Caleb.

They paused and looked at each other.

"Think there'll be a thunderstorm?" Caleb asked.

10

Joseph had an umbrella under his arm. "Looks like it," he said.

"Why don't you take the umbrella?" Caleb smiled.

"Okay. Thanks."

Joseph bounded down the steps and into his car. Caleb waved as he drove off.

The cloudburst gave Joseph an excuse when he was late meeting Derrick at the airport. Traffic was lighter headed back into the city. As he cruised along the parkway, Joseph tapped his fingers on the steering wheel. He felt invigorated by the bright view of the bay and the sun's reflection on the cables of the Cross Island Bridge. Derrick sat next to him, looking silently out at the powerboats in the distance.

A motorcyclist zoomed noisily by on the passenger side. Derrick stuck his arm far out the open window and waved.

"Don't do that, buddy. Bring your arm in."

Derrick hesitated, winced, then obeyed.

"Aren't the boats beautiful?"

A shrug and grimace. Finally a nod.

It was usually like this. Minutes of tension at first, not having seen each other in months, as they readjusted to each other's presence and influence. For several miles they drove in silence, Joseph humming a folk tune Caleb had played on the stereo all weekend. From time to time he glanced curiously across the car at Derrick's profile.

So much was different about him. In just months masculinity had set upon him fiercely. His voice, though still

11

boyish, had turned huffy and deep. Barbs of hair jutted out like warnings on his chin. His biceps, shaped like half-moons, looked hard as metal. He was darker, wider, more solid. The very air around him seemed scented with hormones.

"You're changing fast," Joseph said.

"No, I'm not."

"Yes, you are."

"I feel the same." Derrick looked up and down his arms, mockingly inspecting his palms and the back of his hands. A tiny smile flickered across his face as he pulled a pair of silver-mirrored sunglasses from his shoulder bag. "Yep, the same old Derrick."

Not quite, Joseph thought. Something was new — a quickness in the eyes, a subtle ferocity in his body language. It was as though he expected to be feared and had learned to relish it. His father was no exception.

"What's on the radio in New York?" Derrick asked, punching the buttons on the car radio until he found a hip-hop station. A slow bass beat started over fast drums. Then the drums stopped while the bass swayed like bamboo in a slight wind. When the drums started again, a cartoonish voice began shouting what sounded to Joseph like hostile gibberish. Derrick clapped his hands, his eyelashes fluttering behind his vibrant shades.

"Is this song in English?"

Derrick peered over his glasses. "You square, Pops." He put his arms behind his head and stretched. They were coming off of the bridge. Ahead the expressway stretched into the murky city skyline.

"The big city! I hope the women in New York are ready for me," said Derrick.

"The women here are ready for a lot more than you, I'm afraid."

Derrick flexed his muscles and poked a finger into his father's soft midriff. "Tsk, tsk." He grinned and massaged his own impressive biceps. "Females of New York, look out, boy."

"Oh, please."

"Pop, I can't believe my *muscles*. When I pump iron, it shows up on the Richter scale!" Joseph huffed, but in his heart he was delighted. It was their lifelong private joke, the kid's half-serious bravado. Joseph had always loved Derrick for it. Except now there was a hint of aggression in his joshing, as though he really meant it.

Across the water the Manhattan skyline was becoming clear. The Twins hazy to the south, straight ahead the jigsaw edge in midtown. Over the city a lingering ring of clouds focused a corona of sunlight. It was a funereal effect, fire-red beneath, then lancelike beams of white light. The sight unnerved Joseph. Instinctively he rested his hand on his son's elbow.

"Derrick, I told you about Max Quincy, didn't I?"

"That caterer dude, your big client? No, what happened?"

"You see these guys along the highway that wipe windshields for money? Max liked to let them wash his windshield. Most people say no or turn on their window washers, but Max said yes. Then he'd flash a hundred-dollar bill and say, 'Got change for a hundred? Nope? *Sorry'* and drive away laughing."

"What a jerk."

13

"But Max played his joke on one old man too many times. Out there on the highway, this guy was just waiting for that wise guy in the blue Mercedes to show up again. And one day, sure enough, along comes Max out of the Holland Tunnel, flashing a hundred. 'Yeah, I got change,' the guy says. And he pulls out a cherry bomb—"

"Oh, sweat!"

"He lights it, throws it in Max's lap, and runs away."

"Ruthless!"

"It slides under his butt, and before Max can do anything, it explodes and shreds the base of his spinal column. Thank God he has the use of his hands."

Derrick looked childish and frightened for a moment.

"And he was my biggest account. I did all his media work."

Again, slightly unnerved, Joseph patted his son gently on the shoulder.

"Damn. New York is wild, boy."

They pulled onto a quiet, tree-lined street near Riverside Park. A white-haired jogger passed carefully by. Then a woman on a bicycle with a bouquet of flowers on her handle rack. An elderly woman with a yapping Pekingese chatted with the doorman across the street. Derrick jumped out of the car and grabbed his shoulder bag and suitcases out of the backseat.

"Can you make it?" asked Joseph.

"You kidding? If you want, I can carry this mailbox upstairs too."

"Wait a minute!"

"What's wrong, Pop?"

Joseph had forgotten the *Tailgunner* centerfold Caleb had taped onto his bedroom wall. And now that he thought of it, the stack of *Colt* muscle magazines to be recycled. "Damn," he whispered. The *New York Native,* the special gay pride bulletin on his desk. And in his bookcase — oh, no! *Brother to Brother, Here to Dare, A Boy's Own Story, Being Homosexual, The Creative Homosexual, Gays and the Church, 100 Years of Pride.*

He would have hidden "the evidence" the night before as he always did when Derrick visited, except Caleb had kept him up late talking. On purpose, evidently. And again this morning, kissing, distracting him, making him late for Derrick's flight. Evidently on purpose.

"You want to go get dinner?" he asked.

"Let's drop off the bags first."

"I'll bring up the bags. You wait in the car."

"Dad, my bells are in that bag. I don't want you to have a heart attack."

"That's all right. I missed the gym, and I need the workout."

"Get serious. I'll help you."

"No. You watch the car."

"Just park it."

"Stay in the car, Derrick!" Joseph shouted.

"Forget it!" Derrick got into the car and slammed the door. "I'll be back in a minute."

Derrick watched his father stumble across the street carrying two of his bags. "Don't hurt yourself," he said when his father came back for the heaviest bag. Winded and sweaty, Joseph stopped to rest on the fender of the car. Then he lifted the trunk-size suitcase and lugged it across the street and up the stoop. He pulled the bags into the elevator and then disappeared behind the closing door.

His father was gone a long while, it seemed. Derrick hung his head and sat quietly. A car horn honked behind him. Glancing into the rearview mirror, he saw that strange kid from last summer, the cowboy, walking up the street. He looked away with a start.

Several times last summer Derrick had seen him loitering near his father's house, leaning against the mailbox in his funny snakeskin boots. One day as Derrick and his father arrived home, the cowboy came up to them. He gave Derrick the strangest look and then stepped aside to talk in private to Joseph. As they whispered their business, Derrick mulled and circled, glancing down at those pointy boots stained with water and dust. The cowboy seemed to be scamming his father. His father seemed to reject him. Derrick guessed the boy — his name was Macon Summerscale — was trying to sell his father some marijuana. Still, he felt vaguely bothered and curious. He hated the cowboy. Going upstairs with his dad, he had felt a gusting emptiness inside, as if a sandstorm was stirring in his innards.

Derrick looked up into the rearview mirror again. No, it wasn't the cowboy after all. It was a woman in jeans with a unisex hairdo.

"Damn. I'm seeing things." He sat drumming his fingers on the dashboard, scratching his trace of a mustache, punch-

16

ing the buttons on the car radio. There was news of a police shooting in the Bronx.

Is Pop ever coming back?

Twenty minutes later Joseph came outside and got into the car.

"You want to eat down at the Seaport?" he asked, out of breath. He wiped his brow with a red bandanna and started up the ignition.

"Sure, Pop," Derrick answered. Minutes later they were speeding along Riverside Drive. The clouds had cleared, and the Hudson River basked, smooth-backed like a seal, under a white sun. The scent of fish and sulphur floated in off the water. Derrick stared across the car at his father, who wouldn't look back.

Again he thought of the cowboy, the cloudy eagerness in his eyes, as if Derrick's old dad was his last hope. It wasn't a neutral look on that boy's face, Derrick decided. No drug dealer looks like that. That look contained emotions.

he movie theater was nearly empty. In the movie the porn legend was showering with a plump black woman with large pink nipples. Caleb sat with his foot wedged between two seats near the back of the theater. Earlier he had fallen asleep, perhaps for a half hour, until a noisy orgasm on-screen woke him up. Now he watched the porn legend's flopping penis, soaped up and sliding between the woman's floundering breasts.

Before meeting Joe Grant, Caleb had come every week to the X-rated movie houses around 42nd Street, first out of curiosity, then out of eagerness to see the male sex stars, especially the Legend and the famous "Stiff Man," who could put out a book of burning matches with sperm. He hadn't been to Times Square in a year, and he was disgusted by it now. The women on the screen looked ill, and he had never realized before how ugly the Legend was.

He dropped his foot to the grainy, sticky floor. A portly man in short sleeves was groping his way up the aisle, guiding himself through the dark by the seat backs. He came close, fingers searching, and put a soft hand on Caleb's shoulder. "Excuse me," the man whispered, continuing his way up the aisle. Minutes later Caleb still felt the warm impression of fingers on his skin and was still prodding stiff in his jeans as a result of the man's spice-scented aftershave.

His hands felt dirty. He pulled his underwear from his back pocket to wipe his palms, then accidentally dropped them on the floor. "I'm not picking *those* up," he muttered, pressing the lighted dial on his digital watch. It was after 4 o'clock.

I'd better get home, he thought. His father would be after him to walk the Doberman. It was his kid brother's turn to make dinner tonight. Ted knew how to cook only hot dogs, canned sauerkraut, and spaghetti. Right now his father was sitting down in the recliner in the living room with a cup of coffee, his heart pills, and cigarettes to argue and kvetch with the black anchorwoman on the local evening news.

The train rolled across the Manhattan Bridge. Caleb sat with his feet up, looking out the train window. In the near distance he could see the Brooklyn Bridge running parallel to the train across the river. Three boys his age were clowning in the seats across from him. The tallest, his palm covering his mouth, stretched out his legs on the catercorner seat, his dirty sneakers smudging an Indian woman's dress as his buddy punched him in the shoulder over and over. Caleb's eyes found the boy's slightly hairy ankles, his mus-

19

cular shank, then the small, slanted lump in his crotch. He looked up to find small brown eyes flaring at him, questioning. The tall boy whispered something to his buddy. Caleb turned away and looked out the window, as far up the river as he could until the gray-green water disappeared in an opaque haze of setting sunlight. The train pulled into the first stop in Brooklyn, and the three boys jumped up noisily and left the train.

There was a rustle of boarding passengers — a shift change at work, a scene change in a play. The train suddenly felt more crowded. In the rear of the car, a raspy, resonant voice spoke — an Old Testament voice exhorting the passengers, asking for money, and yet damning them in its hopeful, quiet anger.

"You know you can afford it. You just don't want to give. That's okay with God. 'Cause he know I can make it. I don't need nothin'. You the ones that need somethin'. I'mah see you again. All right."

The voice was coming closer. Caleb turned to see a gray-haired black man, skeletally thin, propelling himself gracefully up the aisle on wooden crutches. His left hand, wrapped around the crutch handle, pinched a metal cup between two free fingers. His voice sounded musical now, punctuated by the rhythm of his swinging body and loose change tinkling like a tambourine in his cup. Caleb looked into the man's bulging, off-white eyes. The stare fixed him, personally, almost intimately, froze and penetrated him. He turned away. The train stopped, and the doors opened. The

20

old man pivoted nimbly on a single crutch and then leapt across the doorway out of the car.

Whenever Caleb spent the weekend with Joseph, they always went shopping on Friday evening. TV dinners, frozen pizza, beer, and chips to last till Monday. A thin black woman with snowy cornrowed hair was always there, begging in front of the market. It wasn't long before she recognized the lovers and figured they were homosexuals. Now every weekend she frowned at Joseph with a wincing scorn, a disapproving mother scowling out of a Freudian dream. At Caleb, though, she could look only with bafflement, a universe of doubt across her broadening face. He offered her money. The first time she took it, her eyes bright with surprise. The next week she pulled her cup away and curled her lip when Caleb held out a fistful of quarters.

The crippled prophet reminded Caleb of that beggar-woman. The man seemed to know all Caleb's secrets; somehow he knew Caleb had just come from a black man's bed. *My brother's bed,* he might have thought. In turn Caleb recalled the night a policeman came to Joe's apartment. When the doorbell rang, Joseph opened it without thinking, expecting the pizza boy. Instead it was a police officer asking about a suspect seen in the vicinity. And there sat Caleb on the sofa in just his white cotton briefs, bare feet up on the coffee table. The officer's nose shriveled like an animal's snout as his lip turned fearfully under his mustache. He stood a moment as if pondering what crime was being committed here, then said good evening and left.

21

"There. Nothing happened, see?" Caleb remembered saying to Joseph, who was much more fearful about their relationship.

Mind your damn business, he thought to no one in particular. It was him and Joe against everyone. There were a few other men, an occasional boy, and a gay woman friend. But mostly it was just him and Joe. Against schoolgirls smacking their Chiclets in their cheeks, brandishing their displeasure that he hadn't noticed their showy halter tops; and straight boys traveling in packs like wild dogs, grabbing their testicles, daring him to look; and beggars and homeless cripples who knew everything, passing judgment out of their burning black corneas.

He had told his dad he was staying with some friends for the weekend, then going straight to work Monday morning. He wasn't sure if the old man had heard him. Regardless, there would be four days' store of suspicion waiting when he got home.

The train pulled into Carroll Gardens. Caleb stood by the door and let the crowd of hurrying, pressing bodies push him off of the train.

When Caleb arrived home, Ted was in the kitchen talking to his girlfriend on the cordless phone. Ted grinned and pointed to the living room as Caleb locked the kitchen door behind him. A pot of spaghetti was boiling on the stove.

"Is that you, Caleb?" a phlegm-filled voice called from the living room. Ted grinned again and shook his head. "Teddy, is that Caleb?" The crepe-paper voice tried its best to shout.

"Yes, Poppy," Caleb shouted back.

"You better walk that goddamn dog. I don't want him pissing on the fucking carpet. You better take care of that animal or I'll kill him."

Caleb walked over to the stove and sniffed the pot of spaghetti and sauerkraut.

I'm really hungry, he thought.

There had never been any doubt about where Joseph would live. He longed to run free, he was queer as he could be, and so it had to be New York. After college (Brown U. in Rhode Island) he rushed back unhesitatingly to the city where he was born. At first, in his awful expectancy, he haunted Times Square at night, thrilled by the galaxy of neon above and the just-as-colorful freaks and foulmouthed whores on the street; then the waterfront, where his blood rippled with fear and his spurred lust found willing bounty.

After fifteen years he was still infatuated with the city. He belonged here; he felt deeply that he did. It was the city that allowed him his gay life with Caleb and, before that, with Macon — hopeless, crazy Macon. New York also afforded him a living as a graphic artist. To Joseph the city was a vast minefield, randomly brutal, as pitiless as God, and that excited him furiously. In the speaking beat of congas on the Lower East Side, in the warlike shouts of partygoers beneath his window near dawn, and in the exhausted faces of half-

24

clothed women lying in heaps in the subway stations, he felt a powerful affinity and sensed the fine essence, for better or worse, of his own quietly rebellious urges.

Much of his urban life, the worst of it, he felt compelled to hide from his son. But the arts and nightlife, the cultural ether of a great town, he was eager to share. Perhaps Derrick was old enough now to enjoy jazz, good film, contemporary art. To Joseph the arts were exploding metaphors for freedom — could an eighteen-year-old appreciate that? Could he talk to his boy about art and hard, grown-up life? With a light eagerness and a prickly apprehension, he planned the time they would spend together "on the town."

Derrick was still curious about the suitcase incident. But soon enough he forgot about it. Surprisingly, he was having too good a time with his old weird dad. And at some point he had to tell Joseph of his plans. He had already told his mother. He wanted to move in, declare residency, enroll at City U., *change his life.* He wasn't here just for the summer. But time enough to talk about that, he thought.

Joseph took him to the Museum of Modern Art. Derrick's favorite was the voluptuous sculpture of a giant green egg that appeared to shift shades and float as he stared at it. *The Headless Scarecrow* exhibit he found agreeably unnerving. He listened as his father talked about the cartoon demigods drawn in colored chalk by a Nigerian artist. "Weird but cool" was Derrick's overall assessment.

After the museum they lunched at Crepes and More Crepes in the plaza beneath Radio City. Derrick tried the lobster and caviar crepes; his father, the Swiss cheese and white rum. When Joseph offered him a sip of vodka, he grimaced and coughed, pretending it was his first time tasting booze. They laughed and traded bites of crepe and talked more about the museum.

And the days went on like this. There was a classic gangster film revival downtown; at night they went to gangster movies, then to the comedy clubs on McDougal Street. They drank liquor and laughed together as adults for the first time ever at jokes spiced with sin and horror.

In the daytime they went shopping. Joseph wanted desperately to impress his son. He bought him new shoes, a diving watch, a black leather jacket. The plan was to whet the kid's taste for the fruits of hard work. But honestly, Joseph was only indulging his boy's whims out of love. He wanted Derrick to know the power he had over his dad.

What Derrick wanted most was the Isoflex device, a handheld isotonic exercise machine he had seen in *Powerlifter* magazine. In a sports emporium near Herald Square, Joseph tried out the Isoflex first, joking with the salesman that he didn't want "the kid" to hurt himself. Failing father struggled proudly with the springs, barely budging the handles, registering forty pounds on the pressure meter.

"Here, Gramps. Let Black Hercules do it." Derrick took the machine, preened for a moment, briskly shook his head, squared his legs, and squeezed the handles. His forearms trembled violently; his triceps shone metallically. Onlookers gathered to watch. Smiling into his father's eyes, Derrick slammed the handles shut. The meter shot up to 300 pounds. He laughed and released, letting the springs burst apart fearsomely. The crowd applauded, and the burly salesman told Derrick he should purchase the heavyweight-level machine. Joseph patted his son on the back to more cheers from the crowd.

"Don't be ashamed, Pop. So you're falling to pieces. I still love you."

Joseph was embarrassed and angry and ashamed of being angry. Up from his belly, pride spit into his throat, making his brow dark and menacing. Derrick eyed him anxiously as Joseph groped for a way to handle his embarrassment. There was a peppermint wrapped in plastic on the dashboard. Joseph grabbed the candy and hurled it childishly across the car, hitting his son in the cheek. Derrick's worried look turned into a starry smile.

"Show-off," said Joseph.

"Rip Van Winkle," Derrick laughed.

It was Saturday morning, and Derrick had the apartment to himself — his father was out at the dentist's. He pulled on his still-damp jockstrap, black jogging shorts, and orange tank top and warmed up for his daily workout. A flurry of push-ups first, then sit-ups and knee bends. Barely winded, he strapped on a pair of ankle weights and did three sets of handstand push-ups, gasping to finish the final set.

"Good!" he said aloud; the ache in his arms meant progress. He set his timer and spent a quarter hour with the

Isoflex, then reset his timer for another quarter hour of shadowboxing.

Bending low, he swung vigorously at empty air with half-open fists. Uppercuts, jabs, eight-punch combinations. *Crouch,* he remembered. *Love the pain. Despise weakness!* Five more minutes. Now, excruciating twelve-punch combinations. "Muthah! Ffff-fuckah!" he cried out. Invisible knives slashed at his triceps. Sweat trickled down his face, into his mouth so he could drink it, into his eyes so they stung badly.

The timer bell went off. "Done!" he shouted, dropping to the floor to lie for a minute at rest.

Now for his yoga breathing. Derrick stood up again briskly. Air through the nose, hands clasped above his head. Thirty deep inhalations. He bit his lip to keep from breathing through his mouth as he badly wanted to. Twenty-three. Twenty-two. His sinuses burned. There was a bursting strain in his gut. Fifteen. Thirteen. *I hate yoga,* he thought. Against his nature, it was tougher than push-ups, jogging, or dead-weights. Seven more. Five. Two.

"Done, damn it!" he shouted. Immediately he pulled off his shirt, using it to wipe the moisture from his armpits. He pinched the barest bit of fat around his ribs and hissed. "Work harder!" he cried aloud, squeezing fist in palm. He sat down on the floor with his legs crossed and breathed exuberantly through his mouth.

A cool, waterlike aggression throbbed inside of him. His lungs worked like emergency surgeons, pumping to restore his energy. He felt an irritation in his crotch and an itch from draining sweat in his armpits. After a moment of painful exhaustion, an ethereal charge coursed through his body like an old knowing river. Slowly his heart and breathing became gentle, normal again.

He stood up and walked onto the terrace. He could see treetops below in Riverside Park and through bright leaves the failing edge of a small dock and a tarred post to which two small rowboats were tied. Derrick had played on the dock as a child, scrambling across planks rickety even then as he held his nose at the stink of dead fish. He looked into the huge sky over the river and remembered fireworks the summer he turned eleven. Even now he could smell lighter fluid and the charring salt scent of beef from the cookout with his father. Derrick stretched his arms high over his head and then went back indoors. He would have a drink, then go for a run in the park. He wanted a closer look at the old sentimental dock.

The doorbell rang while he was in the kitchen. *Who the hell is this?* he wondered. Someone had called earlier and hung up when he answered. He went to the door, calling out impatiently, "Who is it?"

A young male voice answered. "I'm looking for Mr. Grant."

Derrick cracked opened the door. A white youth about his age stood there, dressed in a baseball jersey, sweatpants rolled up his calves, and a black ball cap turned backward on his head. He held a shopping bag.

"I'm looking for Joe Grant," he said. "I have, uh, a package for him."

"I'll take it." Derrick reached out his hand.

29

The boy ignored his open palm and stepped closer to the door. "Can I come in? I work for Joe at Vector Media. I'm trying to get in good. You know, buttering up the boss."

"All right," said Derrick curiously, standing back and opening the door.

"Thanks. I know it's a weird request." Caleb turned the ball cap around on his head as he wiped his sneakers on the welcome mat.

"You're Derrick, right?"

"Right."

"Joe talks about you at work. I'm Caleb."

Derrick gave him a long, doubtful look. In the sunny apartment he could see now that the boy was blond and his eyes a rich and cutting blue. He frowned, then relaxed his expression.

This is my house, Caleb thought. He'd slept in the bed, bathed in the tub, mopped up the kitchen, even decorated the walls. Back on his heels, Caleb posed awkwardly while Joe's kid eyed him almost rudely. He figured it was fair to stare back.

The resemblance gave him a quiet thrill. Before him, half dressed, stood the adolescent image of his man, his lover, Joe Grant. The same tall body that had engulfed him under damp sheets. The dark skin, like polished oak, with an undertint of red, and the contrasting ocher eyes. The rounded jawbone, flowing into oval lips.

Wow, Joe's sperm created this guy!

Lust is very quick. Caleb's eyes came to rest on a protruding dark nipple, then on a droplet running down an

30

etched curve in a triceps. Then on the waistband of a white jock, striking against begging, night-dark skin. He took a breath and smelled vinegarlike sweat in the air. "Tight," he whispered.

"Well, what have you got?" asked Derrick.

"A present for Joe." Caleb reached into his shopping bag. "You into the Red Hot Chili Peppers?"

He pulled out a brand-new compact disc and handed it to Derrick. On the cover the band members were dressed in feathers and bells, like clown princes and circus Indians. Black roses and snake tongues were in the background. *Rock music,* thought Derrick. It had never made sense to him.

"This band is fresh," said Caleb.

Fresh? Derrick looked at the CD again. *This is an acid trip. Contemporary hippies,* he thought. Suddenly he looked up angrily.

"Why you giving this white shit to my father?"

Caleb stepped backward. "Joe likes it," he said, his voice rising in pitch.

Derrick calmed down and handed back the CD. "Yeah, well let's hear it."

"Cool."

Derrick started for the living room, but the white kid walked ahead of him directly to the stereo, knelt down, and without hesitating reached for the switch impossibly hidden under the fuse in the back.

31

"This is great," Caleb said, squatting on the floor as he turned up the volume to maximum.

Fast twangy guitars, insane screaming, and a frenetic, percussive bass made Derrick flinch. It sounded as if the drummer had knocked over his trap set.

"This is wack," he muttered. Rock rhythms always made him think of pogo sticks. In his mind he saw circus Indians bouncing on pogo sticks. Caleb stood up and shook his body loosely, in time to the music, Derrick supposed, though it looked as if the white boy were dangling from a rope.

"Joe likes this," said Caleb. "This is the music revolution. Chili Peppers, Smashing Pumpkins, *Frogstomp*." Derrick's face emptied of expression. Caleb stopped dancing and turned off the music.

"Well, I should be going."

But Derrick was very curious. "What's the rush?" He sat on the sofa and gestured toward the love seat. Caleb hesitated, then sat, crossing his legs at the knee.

"So who the hell are you?" asked Derrick.

"I told you. I'm a friend of Joe's. I work for him. I'm a messenger. But I'm learning computers too. Your dad is teaching me."

"Oh, boy. That's Pop. Every day I have to learn some computer shit. I'm supposed to be on vacation, man. We have a Power Macintosh system in the back."

Caleb almost blurted something, then nodded. "Joe's a nice man," he said, uncrossing his legs. "Sometimes."

"What's he like at work?"

"He's nervous all the time. But he's cool in his own way. He acts younger than his age. Sometimes. Sometimes he acts, you know, old."

"He's always old if you ask me."

"He gets me mad sometimes. And he's selfish and stingy. Plus he's a hypocrite, and he manipu—"

Derrick stared wide-eyed, taken aback. Caleb seemed embarrassed by his outburst.

"You come from Cincinnati?"

"Uh-huh." *How do you know?*

"How do you like New York?"

"Too many faggots."

Caleb twitched both his legs. He stood up, staring keenly.

"I'm kidding," Derrick said.

"I gotta go," said Caleb, his voice hollow and tinny.

"I'll make sure my father gets his present."

Caleb stepped tentatively toward the front door as if he wasn't ready to leave. "What are you doing now?" he asked.

"Out for a run." Derrick jogged in place and jabbed at the air. "You were lucky. Another minute, I'd a *been* gone."

"No problem. I have the keys."

Derrick winced as if he had been stuck with a pin.

"I just didn't want to come in without ringing."

Joe's kid had an owlish expression on his face. *I make him angry,* Caleb thought. He flashed a tiny, fleeting smile as he stepped out the door. "Well, bye. Have a good jog."

33

The cowboy, Macon, thought he was done with this one. He reached out lazily with an open palm as he leaned back against the wall behind the bed.

"What's that for?" asked the man.

"Thirty bucks," Macon drawled. "Like we said."

"Stay awhile. You ain't done yet, anyway."

"I got you off, man." Macon jumped up from the bed and tried to look menacing.

The man laughed. "I said I wanted *some* head. I didn't say how much. I'll be ready for some more in, oh, about a half hour."

"Fuck you, man. I'm gonna put the word out on you. My lover is right downstairs, you know."

The man glared at Macon. Then he reached blindly under the bed. He came up with a crumpled twenty-dollar bill and threw it at Macon's feet.

"We said thirty!"

"Take the twenty and get the fuck out before I call the cops."

"Goddamn you, man. I'm gonna find your mother's grave and piss on it."

The man lunged up violently on the mattress.

"Awright, I'm leaving." Macon grabbed the money and hurried out the door.

"I hope I gave you AIDS, you piece of shit!" the man hollered as Macon bounded down the stairs.

His boyfriend was waiting under the awning of a liquor store. It was thunderstorming, and in his damp sweatpants and summer jacket, Sammy looked irritated and cold.

"What took you so long?"

"The fucker wanted me to stay all night. Then he jacked me out of ten bucks."

"I told you not to go with that freak," said Sammy. "I got a vibe."

The two boys hurried across the street, shoulders hunched under the heavy rain. Going down the stairs to the subway, they clumsily jumped the turnstile just as an almost empty A train pulled into the station.

A heat wave came into the city the next day. Joseph woke up Derrick, and together they drove to the beach. In the car Joseph assumed from Derrick's silence that he was just too sleepy to talk — Derrick hadn't mentioned Caleb's visit.

At the shore Derrick immediately went in the water, but Joseph wanted only to loll in the sand, shooing insects as a cool breeze vied with the warming sun for his body's attention. He closed his eyes to listen to the virile ocean waves. Such lovely sound, all thunder and vapors. More beautiful still was the sound of the backwash, hidden under the crashing-down. The patter of bubbles sliding over pebbles, the ocean punching and caressing the earth over and over — an infinite, self-renewing madness of joy.

Joseph looked out and saw his son jumping and dancing in the waves like a pony. Derrick was far out in the water, at a distance that obscured the maturity he'd recently gained. He could have been fourteen now or twelve, not a young man of eighteen. Running and splashing, he seemed as free as the ocean itself. Derrick swam toward the shore until he could stand knee-deep in the water. Then he looked toward his father, waved, and flipped backward, reminding Joseph of the boy Tadzio playing in the Lido.

If it was possible to love his son too much, then Joseph feared he did. It was the selfishness of his love that disturbed him. He felt owned by his son, and he was happily Derrick's possession. There were nuances, privacies, and silliness about him that only Derrick cared about. There were other things, criminal secrets, intimate quirks that only Caleb knew. Joseph flushed. He worried. Was he a good father? A good lover? Had he ever hurt his son?

Joseph laughed. His life was such lunacy. He looked again out over the ocean. Derrick was waving with one hand and pointing north with the other. He waved back as his boy began walking in waist-deep water to the north, toward the sun. Joseph followed him with his eyes until he disappeared in the glare. Then he rolled over on his stomach, facing seaward. The tide had grown stronger; now the waves were rolling nearer to him. An unusually strong one splashed salty droplets in his mouth. He rolled over on his back, shading his eyes with his forearm. He wanted to clear his mind of worry. He was so happy to have Derrick here. He was filled with love, and right now that was all he wanted to feel.

Derrick had walked nearly a half mile from where his father lay resting in the sand. He was looking for a crowd of beachgoers where he might find a girl to talk to. His father had parked near the most isolated stretch of shore, but to Derrick going to the beach meant noisy crowds, flying beach balls, and rows of sunbathing women.

He walked and walked. He could see the forest of colored beach umbrellas, not terribly far now. Cold water splashed over his feet. The sand was wet as soup, leaving soggy, short-lived footprints. He pressed his heels into the mud, then stepped back and watched the depression fill with water and disappear. He turned and looked to the horizon, listening to the brash, beautiful cry of the ocean, the counterpoint of crashing, rolling waves coming from all around him. So beautiful. He started walking faster. He wanted to get away from his father and find some women.

He looked up and saw a young white boy, perhaps ten or eleven, coming toward him on the beach. The boy's feet were caked with dried sand, and he held a red-and-yellow kite by a short string. Derrick stopped walking and watched the youngster, who glanced up at him briefly and continued on. The kite floated sedately on the breeze, well-behaved, casting a black shadow on the boy's shoulders. Derrick turned and stared at his back. The boy reminded him of Caleb, which annoyed him, but he felt also something hotter and more distant. A searing thought possessed him, the memory of a child's brutal death, and his skin flared with a bruising anger.

He began running back toward his father until he had passed the boy with the kite, who smiled sunnily as he ran past. Then he stepped into the ocean, splashed foam over his head, and strode knee-deep in the water until he could see his father lying in the sand. He came near quietly and looked down on him. His face was garnished with gleaming grains of sand, and the sun cast diagonal shadows along his nose and cheek. Derrick shook the wetness out of his hair and dropped down on the blanket, shivering with an aggressive silliness.

"Why did you park so far from civilization?"

Joseph brushed a spot of sand from his upper lip. "I like it here."

"Why you just lie here in the sand? Go in the water," he commanded.

"I'm relaxing."

"You look like a dead dolphin that washed up out of the water."

"Grown-ups need to relax."

"Bull. What, you have stress or something?"

"Leave me alone."

Derrick rubbed wet sand off his toes. *No women for miles,* he thought. "Are you dreaming about Caleb?"

Joseph sat up briskly on his blanket.

"What did you say?"

"Forget it, Pop." Derrick stood up and walked away. He turned around and called back to his father. "I'm gonna go find some females!"

aleb's father had been at him all day about coming in late last night. His bedroom smelled like dirty socks. "Where's the money you owe me, you *patza*? I want you to go to the liquor store and the market." Caleb ignored him and went up to his room, slamming his door behind him.

He was watching MTV when his telephone rang. It was Joseph, hollering about gay whatnot and his kid and why did he come to the apartment. Caleb tossed the receiver down on his blanket. When Joseph stopped yelling, he picked the phone back up.

"I wanted to surprise you," Caleb said in a sweet voice. "Did you get the CD?"

"Yes, baby, and thanks. But you *can't* come over."

"Why not?"

"The situation is too complicated."

"I'll say it's complicated. Your own son hates gays."

There was a loud thump over the receiver. Joseph put down the phone and went away for a moment. Caleb heard him talking to someone.

"What was that?" he asked when Joe came back on the phone.

"Nothing. Derrick dropped something. And he does *not* hate gays."

"If you say so, Joe." There was a loud thump again. Caleb lay back on his bed with the telephone caught between his chin and shoulder, cleaning his fingernails with his Boy's Club card.

"Don't you think I miss you?" asked Joseph.

"No, I don't. I think you just miss screwing me."

"Stop it. I hate not seeing you."

"Great, Joe."

"I tell you what. Why don't you take tomorrow off? With pay. Go to the beach. Tan that little fanny for me."

Caleb didn't answer.

"Caleb?"

"If you say so, Joe," he said in a soft voice and hung up.

He doesn't fool me, Caleb thought. His old granny lover was too cheap to give him a day off for nothing. Joe didn't want him in the office tomorrow, and Caleb was certain why.

He's bringing that son of his to the office.

Caleb turned off his television. He felt overheated and restless. His lover was cheating on him. *That doesn't really make sense,* he reconsidered. But he decided to go to work anyhow and catch Joe in the act.

He slept in late the next morning and had a brief yelling match in the bathroom with his father, who assumed he had been fired. After riding the D train in from Brooklyn, he

41

enjoyed a casual breakfast of pita bread with tomatoes and cheese and a pot of iced coffee at an Indian restaurant on East Houston Street.

Someone had left the morning paper at the table across from him. Caleb waited until the waitress stepped into the kitchen and then snatched it. On the front page were photos of a mass demonstration on the steps of Police Plaza. Just days before, a police officer had shot a Hispanic youth in his living room in the Bronx. He read the headline story as he finished his iced coffee. Then he folded the newspaper and stuffed it into his back pocket. He would talk about it later with Joseph, who was always going on and on about city corruption, police brutality, and all such other adult things.

He chatted with the dark-skinned waitress and paid his check, leaving a two-dollar tip. Then he stepped outdoors and walked briskly toward Avenue A and Eighth Street, the location of Joseph's computer graphics company, Vector Media.

Joe Grant had formed Vector Media (originally Victoria Graphics) ten years ago with his partner, Victor Quincy, a teaching assistant in art when Joseph was in college. Their first business client was Victor's brother Max, who owned a chain of steakhouses in Queens and also published a restaurateur's magazine featuring tips on sidestepping health regulations. Max hired brother Victor to design the magazine and all of his print advertising. As a freelance graphic artist, Joseph had built a list of contacts among minority service agencies of the city of New York. With the help of a pitch from Max at the commercial bank, their small printing and graphics company survived a shaky start-up phase.

Joseph became an eager if unlikely entrepreneur. Though his own taste in art was somewhat highbrow — on weekends he haunted the likes of the Vorpal Gallery and the Stevenson, specializing in African art in SoHo — he enjoyed creating art that was less exclusive. In not much time he learned to blend purist and pop elements into a striking commercial style. And under pressure from Derrick's mother to pay child support, he became compulsively efficient at the mundane aspects of the business — deadlines, advertising, discounts, billing. His clients were uniformly pleased.

Later he brought on the Theater Art Society, a charitable group that sponsored gaudy fund-raising dinners and arts events for booze- and guilt-addled aristocrats. Joseph won an award for designing the Art Society's logo and now did all of its invitations, posters, and announcements. It proved a fruitful association as he extended his client network to include other private arts foundations, which in turn led to some political campaign work. When Victor Quincy died of alcoholism and hepatitis, Joseph cut his prices to keep brother Max as a client.

Business thrived in the 1980s, and at one point Joseph had working for him a staff of eight. Since Max Quincy's retirement, there were only four — two designers, a messenger-janitor, and Caleb, who began working for his lover part-time in the fall and full-time since the start of summer.

The company was located in a somewhat run-down, white, brick-faced, five-story building on Eighth Street, west of

Tompkins Square Park. Gangs of homeless youth often blocked the building's entrance by day. Today there was just one wiry female waif, no older than thirteen, in a tattered leather jacket, sitting glumly on the stoop rolling a pair of dice. In her blond hair were strands of green dye. She glared angrily as Caleb sidestepped the dice but stepped on her drooping leather belt. He apologized, then punched the buzzer, pushed open the heavy front door when it unlocked, and went quickly up the stairs. When he got to the top floor, he paused outside the office and listened.

Inside someone was enduring a fit of sneezing. *Sounds like Douglas is dying,* he thought. He opened the white pine door and entered the sunny office, a converted painter's studio. He was right. Douglas Seasons, the senior systems operator, was digging vulgarly into his nostrils with a pink handkerchief.

"Try rose hips, Douglas. Vitamin C." Caleb spoke vigorously, excited to be in the office. He was the owner's lover, after all, which made him a prime object of ass kissing.

"It's the garbage," said Douglas. "I swear they haven't picked up the garbage in the East Village in a month."

"It's your imagination, Douglas," offered Dolores Wilder, a black woman in her late twenties and the newest staff member besides Caleb. Dolores was Joseph's creative assistant, specializing in three-dimensional software and color animation.

"Well, speaking of health, how are you, Caleb?" asked Douglas. "Joseph called this morning and said you wouldn't be in. He thought we might have to get a sub from Manpower. Lots of stuff going out today, you know. I told him, 'Hell no, I'll just run Paulie into the ground.' "

"There's nothing wrong with me. Joe said I was sick?"

"Well, I just assumed…"

"He said I could take the day off." Caleb sighed.

"Oh. Then why are you here?"

"It's personal, Douglas."

"Oh, personal? Come. Talk." Douglas waved for Caleb to come over.

"I don't think I want to hear this," said Dolores, turning back to her worktable, where she was measuring a layout by hand with a point ruler. Caleb walked over and sat on the edge of Douglas's desk.

"So, how are things in paradise?"

"Um…fine." Caleb gestured meaninglessly, playing for sympathy. He really did like Douglas, because Douglas liked him and had never resented his being there. "All right."

"I'll bet you're disappointed you two can't spend his vacation together."

"I think he knows that. He wants to make it up to me."

"You're a dear child, Caleb. It's so obvious why he loves you. He is crazy about you, you know."

"Yes, I guess so."

"Well, you know he only sees his son two or three times a year. He's trying to be a good daddy."

"I met his son the other day."

Douglas looked surprised. "You did? Where?"

45

"At Joe's apartment. He looks just like Joe. Only young."

"I've known Derrick for a long time. He's not very much like Joe. No, he and his father are very different."

"How do you mean?" Caleb became very interested.

"Oh, I can't…"

Caleb glanced at Dolores, then came around and knelt by Douglas's chair.

"Come on, Douglas."

"Don't you tell Joseph I said this."

"You know I wouldn't."

"Well, Derrick takes after his mother, Racine, who is just like Joe's mother, Grace. It's all very gay-oedipal. Derrick has no inhibitions. He sees, and he just *goes"* — Douglas accented his voice — "you know what I mean?" He snapped his fingers. "He's a tough boy."

"Yeah, I could see that about him."

"Oh, I've seen it too. But let me finish. You see, you are the same way, Caleb. You're very willful for such a young person. It's your chutzpah. That turns Joe on. Believe me, I know the type of man he likes. He respects strong women — look at Dolores over there—"

"I can hear you," said Dolores.

"Did you remember to turn on the tape recorder?"

"I just don't want you to say the wrong thing."

Douglas pursed his lips and waved her away. "And he loves girlish boys — pardon me — with lots of balls and chutzpah, just like you, Caleb. Believe me, you're giving him exactly what he wants."

"Very good, Dr. Ruth," piped in Dolores.

Douglas turned, addressing her. "Would you agree that Joseph is very excited by aggressiveness combined with femininity? You should have seen him during *Dynasty*. He *worshiped* Alexis. He was so embarrassed, I was the only one he would talk to about it. I swear, Gloria Steinem is like his personal guru."

"Glenn Close too."

"Oh, don't get him started. *The World According to* — what was her name?"

"Jennie something?"

"I know Joe is a feminist," said Caleb tentatively, feeling lost in the conversation. The only name he had recognized was Gloria Steinem.

Dolores swung her chair around to face them both. "It's the contradiction. Paradox excites him. You can see it in his painting." She swung back around and returned to work.

"Isn't she just brilliant? I have to start kissing your ass, Dolores, in case he decides to marry you."

Caleb blanched. Dolores turned her head and smiled wickedly.

"Don't worry, Caleb."

"I'm not worried, Dolores."

"He's *not* worried, Dolores," said Douglas.

"That's what I said. Don't worry."

"You don't have to worry about her, Caleb. She only fucks billionaires."

"That's me. Just a gigolo in drag."

"If Joe ever falls for another woman, I guarantee it will be a radical feminist lesbian. She'll have a short haircut, black high-top sneakers, pink polka-dot culottes, and a raggedy white cotton tank top with black leather wrist bands."

"And she'll be a member of the Communist Party," said Dolores.

Douglas nodded and laughed. "And she'll play bass guitar in a rhythm-and-blues band."

"Now, that's your competition, Caleb," said Dolores.

"But if she's a lesbian?" Caleb asked. Douglas and Dolores both looked at him and laughed. He stood up and turned away. Old people were irritating him generally these days. There were times when he thought of them as an alien species.

Just as Dolores and Douglas stopped laughing, the door slammed open. A dark young man in a blue denim jacket and jeans entered, wiping his forehead with a paper towel.

"Caleb, where the hell you been? You were supposed to make two deliveries uptown. I been busting my heinie all morning."

Douglas gestured to Caleb not to speak. "Caleb had a reaction to some medication, Paulie. He can't work today. I cleared it with Joseph." Paulie hadn't yet realized that Caleb was Joseph's lover, and for this reason Douglas thought he was slow.

"Take yourself a break, Paulie. You have to go to Queens this afternoon, and you have two pickups in the Wall Street area."

Paulie grabbed a soda from the refrigerator. "There's extra cops on all the trains. They're expecting trouble."

"Well, they asked for trouble. They shot an innocent fourteen-year-old," articulated Dolores.

"I agree with you," said Paulie, sitting down on the sofa. "It makes things dangerous for everybody."

Dolores slapped her pencil down on her desk. "Now I'm too angry to work," she said. "Caleb, honey, play some music for me, will you? I can't concentrate with all this aggravation."

"Glad to, Dolores." Caleb wasn't angry at her anymore. He sat down at the old upright piano in the corner and began playing the Rachmaninoff prelude that his mother had taught him when he was twelve.

"You're so talented, Caleb," said Douglas.

"What's that you're working on, Dolores?" asked Paulie.

"The layout for the wheelchair services fund-raiser. You know, the ramp nuts."

"Ever hear the words 'PC,' honey?" chimed Douglas.

"Oh, please. I'm doing their fucking layout for half price. What more do you want?"

Paulie jumped in. "Speaking of wheelchairs, you won't believe who I saw downtown. Max Quincy."

"Poor guy," said Caleb, the only one in the office who had liked Max. A loud and aggressive man, Max had always greeted him with a burly embrace and a dirty joke.

"Get this. I saw him at a bus stop on Fifth Avenue. A black bus driver was helping him onto the bus."

"That's ironic," said Caleb.

"It'll be more than ironic if we all lose our jobs."

"Joe told me don't worry," said Caleb, glancing at Paulie. Joe had confided to him that he might let Paulie go.

There was a lull in the conversation as Dolores and Douglas worked, Paulie sipped a Pepsi Cola, and Caleb played a slow, blurry blues at the piano, his hands close in the center of the keyboard. The front door opened, and Joseph entered with Derrick a step behind him.

"Hi, Joe," said Caleb brightly.

"What's up, boss?" said Paulie.

"Hello, everybody. I'd like you to meet my son. Derrick, you know Douglas. Everyone else is new. That's Dolores, and over there is Paulie." He paused and looked at Caleb, who stood up from the piano bench. "By the piano, that's Caleb."

"The boss's son, huh?" said Paulie, jumping up from the sofa and holding out his hand. "I have to get on your good side."

"Good to meet you."

"How long you gonna be in town?"

"Maybe a month."

"Cool. We gotta hang, man. Go out to a ball game. You like baseball?"

"I like women more than baseball."

"I hear that. Well, I gotta run." Paulie picked up a portfolio. "Douglas, I'll be back about 3 o'clock. Nice to meet you, Derrick." He slapped Joseph's back as he left.

"So, Derrick, I hope you're ready to do some work," Douglas joked.

"Hell no, Douglas."

50

"Derrick," said Joseph, "I want you to see the new Apple QuickTime software. Dolores, show him the animation sample."

"Come on over here, young brother. I have some interesting things to show you." Dolores led Derrick to the high-end graphics terminal in the back room.

"It's so refreshing to have children in the office," said Douglas.

"How are things?" Joseph asked Douglas.

"Fine. Don't think twice about it. You're on vacation."

Joseph looked over at Caleb, who had sat back down and was silently fingering the piano keys.

"How are you, Caleb?"

"Caleb's not the only prize little peacock at Vector Media anymore," chimed Douglas.

"I'm fine," said Caleb. Derrick and Dolores were laughing in the back room. Joseph walked over and stage-whispered over Caleb's shoulder.

"I thought you were taking the day off."

"Ah. Caught you, didn't I?"

"Caught me? Are you nuts?"

Caleb glanced at Douglas, who was watching intently.

Derrick came back into the room excited. "Dad, that software is *fierce*. I want to learn it."

Joseph stepped back and smiled falsely. "Great. We'll come in one night next week. Dolores, could I take a look at your layout?"

Derrick walked over to Caleb by the piano. "Whazzup, chump?" he said.

Caleb bristled and looked down at the keys.

"Can't you tell when somebody's kidding?"

Derrick came closer, forcing Caleb to move over on the bench. The nerves in Caleb's face flashed. *Too many faggots,* he remembered.

"I thought you said you worked here." Derrick tinkled the piano in the bass register. "This what you call work?"

"Joey gave me the day off. With pay." A touch of feyness slipped into his voice. He crossed his legs girlishly on the piano bench. "You know, there are things I could tell you."

"What, about how you're getting over on my father?"

"It comes with the color," Caleb mumbled.

"What did you say?"

"Nothing."

"Tell me what you said, punk," Derrick whispered.

"I didn't say nothing." Caleb shook his head tiredly. He looked over his shoulder. Joseph was staring at him. "I think your father is waiting for me. I mean for you."

Derrick hovered over Caleb, then smiled coldly and turned away.

"Let's go, Pop!"

"Wait downstairs for me," said Joseph.

Derrick scowled at Caleb. Then he strutted out the door and down the stairs.

"Bye, Derrick," called out Douglas.

"Hurry up, Pop," Derrick called back.

Joseph hurried over to Caleb. "What did you say to him?"

"Nothing!"

52

CUSTODY

Headache. Joseph's temples throbbed over his predicament. The two men in his life, his son and his lover, were headed at each other like trains. Both refused to do what he wanted. Derrick refused to mind his business, and Caleb was more exasperating than ever!

How did it happen? Joseph was as gay a man as ever lived, his blood pure lavender, his heart pink as a tulip. He was ecstatically homosexual. How did he end up with a kid to complicate his life so impossibly? It wasn't so unlikely. The act in which Joe's son was conceived was aimed more at the man in the next room than at the woman who thought she had seduced him.

He was Derrick's age, a careless and undecided sophomore in college, when Racine, Derrick's mother, came to him at breakfast and told him she was pregnant. The word made him shudder. It didn't even sound like an English word, more like an Eskimo dialect. *Preg-nant.*

All term he stumbled around campus in penitent shock as Racine's terrifying belly grew bigger and bigger. He wasn't even sure why he had slept with her. And how stupid not to protect himself. Perhaps if he had known anything about women, if he had ever wondered about their bodies, like most young men, he might have thought of contraception. It wouldn't have seemed such an outlandish, alien idea.

To this day he suspected she had hypnotized him. Her eyes were very quick; she had circled him. And she seemed to know instinctively what he needed. In her bright dashiki, with her knowledge of the proper poets, she reassured Joseph among the other black students on campus, with whom he felt suspect and uncomfortable. She appeared to like his paintings and him as well. Hands on his neck, she baited his thoughts on Dr. Kissinger's immoral policies or the U.S. role in Africa. "Radical at work," she teased as he clasped his hands in the afternoon and formed his ideas on the nature of power. Joseph was so innovative in his contempt for tyranny.

In time she grew bolder. With long fingernails she flicked his earlobes, pinched his palms, scratched the skin around his neck. One early evening they kissed in the dark woods near campus. With determined arms Racine drew him into enveloping folds of softness. There were questions and questions for Joseph. Her body was mysterious and warm, though not appealing to his genitals.

The sex itself was an act of obedience. Later he thought it was an act of slavery. The first night a single Tensor lamp illuminated the wall in his room like a spotlight. Dilated pupils exaggerated the bright effect. Slightly dizzy, Joseph watched the shadows on the wall as Racine swiftly undid her bra. It would be a radical act, he thought. Poignant, vulgar, aesthetically severe, and this was reason enough to do it.

It was also an act of revenge on the soccer player Reggie in the room next to his — tall Reggie, handsome, sleek, and black as olives, who all semester had assaulted Joseph's nerves by fucking his girlfriend to distraction behind centimeter-thick plywood walls. Night after night, Joseph's legs had spasmed under his sheets as Reggie's girl cried out her pleasure. Now it was his turn. He wanted Reggie to hear him making love. But Racine stretched beneath him to absorb his strength, squeezing his neck and whispering. Too quietly. Joseph shouted her name. She answered by shouting his. *Joey!*

He fell into her, incited to frenzy by the weak, bulbous flaps, the gurgling redness staring him in the face. And angry, squinting, furious at Reggie, jouncing and grunting away night after night and *ignoring him*! Joseph bumped his head against the wall. *Can you hear me, Reggie?* Sheets were on the floor, fingernails ripped through the knots in his hair. Eyes closed and gasping, he thrust forward blindly. *I can fuck too. Can you hear me?* A spurt, seconds sooner than he thought, and young gay Joseph was caught.

Two months later she told him she was pregnant.

"I can't marry you," he said.

"Nobody asked you to."

"I'll support the baby."

She laughed. "You're damn right, you will."

A year later, in their senior year, Joe and Racine with their baby Derrick sat on the porch of the red row house where they lived on trial as a family. She rocked their infant in her arms, whispering in pig English while Joseph's cheeks trembled. He closed, opened, closed his fists. Silently he was trying to communicate with her, this woman to whom he was now so shockingly, irrevocably bound. Racine looked up from the child in her arms and saw his awful expression.

"Tell the truth, Joseph. Do you want a baby?"

"I didn't expect this."

"Tell the truth now."

"I don't."

Racine lay the infant down preciously in the bassinet. Then she reared up like a sudden spring storm and darkened the porch.

"Well, you got one, understand? You have a baby, and you are no poor nigger. You got an education." She pointed out past the hills. "Now you go get a job. This is your son, you understand? You run off from this child, and no matter where on earth, I — look at me, Joseph — I will come get your black ass."

Her words ricocheted in Joseph's mind but had a steadying effect. The trembling in his cheeks slowed. He appeared to relax. Racine eyed him with satisfaction, her point made evidently. She picked up the child and gently rested him in his father's arms.

After they graduated she moved to Cincinnati, taking Derrick. Joseph went to New York and began his life as a painter and computer artist. He saw his son only once a year at first, though by the time the boy was four, Joseph would spend several weeks a year in Ohio. He paid his child support on time and gave Racine no reason to complain. She never married, but she did advance quickly in her career of chemical research. Joseph visited in Cincinnati when Derrick turned six years old, and Racine had a new demand to make of him. She wanted him to take custody of their son. She had received a medical fellowship to travel and study in the Ivory Coast, and she couldn't take a young child with her.

Father and mother had a hot, terrible argument. That was never their arrangement! shouted Joseph. He didn't know the first thing! It wouldn't be good for the boy. She was so irresponsible.

"Oh, I'm irresponsible?" Racine snapped back, her voice as clear as a jazz trumpet. She was using that Virginia sass that always made Joseph nervous. But he came back with loudness and fury this once, despite his firing nerves.

"You're the boy's mother. No court in the country would let you just run off to Africa. You can't just wake up one morning and give up custody of your son."

"We can go to court if you want to, Joseph. We can go to court, and I can get double the support payments. Then I'll put him in private school."

"It's impossible!"

"Why is it so impossible? What do you have to do?"

Joseph rested his fists on his hips. He felt cornered and desperate and terribly excited; all of his apprehensions vanished. "Racine, I'm gay," he blurted. "I'm a homosexual." His knockout blow. He expected her to be stunned.

"Oh, don't give me that mess." She waved her hand dismissively. "I...I *knew* you were going to bring that up."

"What, do you think I'm lying?"

"Joseph, I have known from the day we met that you were a homosexual. What has that got to do with any damn thing?"

Joseph reeled backward. How had she known? Had he really even known himself in school? He turned away from her in gloom for a moment, then turned back and looked her in the face.

"I have a lifestyle," he muttered.

"What you have is a six-year-old son. You just have to give up your *life-style*" — she broke the word in half in her mouth — "until I get back from my fellowship."

"Did you tell him?"

"No, I didn't tell him, in case you turned out even more selfish than I thought."

Joseph's head was pounding like cannon fire. Racine was right. His sex life in New York wasn't going very well. He hadn't found a man he wanted to love, though he'd tried. For years it was bar after bar, meeting someone perhaps one in a hundred times. Naively he still looked forward to every weekend, but the weekends passed with him standing alone under disco lights, inhaling sweat until last call for booze. Shaking his shoulders in time to machine beats that didn't really move him, not wanting to appear desperate to any potential tricks scoping him out from the shadows. From the bars he moved to the big ballrooms, the Roxy and Crisco Disco. Dancing by himself, perhaps rubbing against the ass of a college student who didn't object. But rarely talking to anyone. Something vague and nameless held tight onto his voice and stopped him from approaching men, and he always left the ballrooms alone.

His fourth year in New York, he discovered the underground clubs in the East Village. A painter friend had introduced him to the scene. Avenue B and east. Eerie, ambient hellholes, jazzy basement firetraps with bomb-shelter lighting and ink-soaked walls years deep in radical or obscene graffiti. An atmosphere opposed to all things normal. Normality was tyranny, so Joseph liked that. Just walking to the clubs was dangerous. Even more so, leaving them near dawn. And though Joseph never spoke to the drag queens and pretty people who shouted and danced, laughed and screamed, waved their hands and flashed their teeth and rings, just being there he felt rebellious. Sniffing cocaine in the bathrooms, his spirit resonating to raucous, airy music, he reveled in the aesthetic of danger. Imagined danger in the clubs and the real danger of walking the streets of Alphabet City so late or so very early. Glimpsing, as he walked, the pale Spanish boys standing wraithlike in doorways or milling in small gangs under dreary streetlamps. They returned his excited glances with cold, inscrutable expressions. Stoned and exhausted, Joseph couldn't distinguish curiosity from menace. He walked past the boys not too quickly, trying not to appear afraid, not daring to reveal his lust, and hailed a cab to take him home. This was his freedom, he cherished it, and now he was being asked to give it up.

Joseph and Racine argued for days. She shouted, pointed her finger, and cursed, and he withered under her persistence. At one point he stopped raising his voice. Quietly he told her about the gay dance clubs and about his lonely artist's life in New York. She knew she had won him over. Perhaps she also knew, as he was beginning to know, that all their shouting had never been an argument at all but primal therapy for Joseph, the thrashing and screaming needed to begin a transformation.

They stood in the bedroom, Joseph exhausted, Racine still talking. Though needlessly now, for Joseph had finally agreed. Derrick ran into the room and jumped up on the bed, playing with the atomic space robot his father had bought him for his birthday. Joseph picked up his boy in his arms and sat down.

"Derrick, I want to ask you something."

"Go ahead, Dad." He didn't look at either of his parents, still preoccupied with the space toy's hidden compartments.

"Your mother and I would like you to come live with me in New York for a while."

"I'm going to be traveling in Africa, honey. Doing research? Would you like to live with your father and your grandmother until I come back?"

"How long?" asked the boy.

"A long time, Derrick," said Joseph. "At least two years."

"You know your mother and father love you, don't you, honey?"

64

Derrick's eyes darted back and forth from his mother to his father. He flicked up the helmet guard on his space robot and peered inside.

"I know. It's okay," he said. He jumped out of Joseph's arms and ran into the backyard.

Racine peered through the venetian blinds to the yard, where her child ran about with his space robot over his head.

"Don't ever tell him you're gay, Joseph."

Joseph didn't answer. He was thinking of the day when his son would know that he *was* gay, no matter what he told. He felt at once the weight of the years to come, his eternal burden of secrecy. Couldn't he just send more money for the child? Racine turned to face him, reading his gnarled expression with utter clarity.

"You keep that a secret, you hear me?"

"I don't see any other choice, Racine."

"You know, Joseph, you don't know your child at all. He's going to change your whole world around."

Of course she was right. Back in New York with custody of his six-year-old, Joseph found his whole life changed. He had never been much for neatness. Now he had to straighten up his apartment and shop and wash and not put things off. He had to do his best always. And he was no longer invisible in his privacy and loneliness.

At the dinner table his first night in New York, Derrick sipped milk from his bowl of frosted cereal, mashing the soggy flakes with his spoon. "You're a good cook, Dad," he said approvingly. Then he stood up and walked all around the apartment, prying and peeking behind doors and curtains as if looking for a stowaway.

"You live by yourself?" he observed.

"Yes."

"I wouldn't want to live alone."

That first night Joseph read to his boy from his own favorite boyhood novel. Derrick listened with glowing attention, curled like a mollusk under his bedsheet, to the fantastic details of Mr. Barrie's *Peter Pan.* By next morning at breakfast he had imagined a sequel. (There had to be one, he insisted, like *Return of the Ghost, Star Wars,* and *Son of Cosmic Warrior.*) In *Pan II* Peter still slept in trees. To keep cool in the summer, he slept on just a hanging leaf. Derrick invented games to test Peter's mettle. How many miles could he fly between the beat of a hummingbird's wings? Five right after breakfast. Ten and back on his best day. Now he was ready to fight his new enemy, the Spirit Ninja, who existed in two dimensions and could be killed only if struck at once in both.

"How do you like that?" sang Derrick in a voice that made Joseph think of fruit punch and sugar crystals.

Derrick was a blabbermouth. He yakked and yakked away, sharing with his father his babyish philosophy or the trivia of his life. Joseph was sure he had inherited the trait from Racine. As for the stomping feet and the private fits of mean-ingless laughter, spinning, blind with innate ecstasy, that must have come from the mother's blood too. From his study Joseph listened in delight to the unrelenting prattle, energy, and noise. Growing inside himself he felt a new love, more profound than mere biology.

Derrick stayed with his grandmother Grace in the Marcus Garvey Houses in Brooklyn. Joseph went to his mother's every evening to have dinner, take his son for a walk, supervise his homework, and put him to bed. Weekends belonged to the boy, as Grandma Grace had church obligations. Soon Joseph was caught up in the immutable rhythms of fatherhood. This felt strange and relentlessly pressing and caused him anxiety. Still, he had only a few regrets. Sex was harder to find. After putting his child to bed, he occasionally went out to bars, the better lit ones now, not the alluring hellholes anymore. He stayed off the streets and piers late at night. For the sake of his boy, Joseph sacrificed the freedom to risk his life.

It was during these years that death came to stay awhile in the city, armed with its microscopic masterwork. Had it been an army instead of a bug, the capital would have sounded an alert. Had it come all at once, the whole city might have died of panic. But death this time came slowly and lazily. It seeped as glue drips. It hurt like a slow, slow roll in a bed of needles.

Joseph was careful not to share a glass, a fork, or a spoon with his young son. Could he even hug him? Public spokesmen were reassuring. *If it were airborne, we'd all be dead already. If it were in sweat—* But they said other things that were doubtful. *Only one in ten will die. You can't get it if...* Keep it moving in one direction, one expert hypothesized. Divide the world into bottoms and tops. It was the undecided or the greedy ones, bottom one night, top the next, who broke the chain and sent *whatever it was* spreading the other way. Joe took this tempting advice one night. *Oh, that big fat ass was good,* then stopped and wondered and became terrified and prayed it wasn't too late.

He decided it couldn't be on the skin, that made sense, or, *yes, we'd all be dead already.* Relieved, he hugged his boy lovingly. But teaspoons and plates were something else. Picnics became finicky things, Joseph rubbing alcohol on his fingers, wary of stray paper cups. Not knowing what was killing gay men, he was relieved that Derrick lived with his grandmother. For a year he never once used the bathroom there.

Joseph met a man — David — through a mutual acquaintance in a piano bar under the 59th Street Bridge. It was a rare Friday afternoon when he allowed himself to get moderately drunk. David was in his late fifties. As the piano man began an old tune by Billie Holiday, David squeezed a lemon into a shot of whiskey and told Joseph, after listening to him yap and preen about Derrick for an hour, that he too once had a son but had one no longer. His boy, Domingo, had changed his legal name after finding men's magazines in his father's closet. David knew neither his name nor his whereabouts now.

"To purify himself, he told me. 'I have to *purify* myself.' " David bit down on an edge of lemon, then dropped it in his lap. He ran a finger around the top of his drink glass wistfully. "He was twenty-five years old then. And he still whined like he was twelve. A snot-faced—"

"That's awful," said Joseph.

"That was the last I heard from him. Twelve years ago."

"Did you love your boy?"

"I loved him dutifully. I would have done anything for him."

"I know what you mean."

"I loved him very much when he was a child. We used to go *fishing*." David laughed as if the image of himself in rubber hip boots was preposterous. "When he started to date girls, I began to distance myself. I knew it was only a matter of time."

"Before what?"

"Before he figured out his dad was queer. I was always afraid his mother would tell him. At the most maliciously opportune moment. On her deathbed or on mine. I'm sure she was waiting until she couldn't have possibly hated me more and couldn't have better savored the moment. In any case" — David now looked epicly sad — "I always knew it was inevitable. And then those damn magazines. Some tasteless imitation of Tom of Finland. I'd forgotten they were up there. Domingo was looking for his old high school yearbook."

"I'm very sorry," said Joseph.

"Let me ask you," David said urgently. "What will you do when your darling seven-year-old, all this sweetness and light of your life you've been telling me about, grows up and calls you a *maricón* to your face?"

Joseph flinched at that word *maricón. Mighty Kong.* He remembered it as the nastiest utterance in the vocabulary of

69

the Puerto Rican boys in the Marcus Garvey Houses where he grew up, held in reserve for the last round of cursing each other out. As a boy he didn't know what it meant in Spanish, but he could tell from the sound of it — the contemptuous downstroke on the slicing, final syllable — that it was something exceptionally bad, much worse than *chinga* or *tu madre come grande bicho.* The kids could tolerate those paltry slurs, but *maricón*! It always started a fight.

Joseph's face turned as gray and fearful as the saddest undertones of piano blues. The piano man, filled with scotch, was playing things he was too young to know. Perhaps he thought he was talking with Billie Holiday in her grave. Joseph thought of the magic in his son's voice, his unrestrained affection, his imagination. Still, a fear was born that evening in a nook of Joe's heart. A lasting fear of his own child.

"I've never known," David started again. He paused to smile at the intense interest on Joseph's face. "I've never known if it was my lifestyle or my emotional distance that made Domingo hate me. Do you watch the Bergman movies? *Autumn Sonata*? That bloody screaming. You can hurt your child without trying, you know, just by living your life. I became so afraid when I saw him growing up. I wanted to abort the whole business while he was still too young to know. I wanted out. To disappear forever."

Joseph couldn't bear to hear any more. But he felt monumentally grateful. He shook David's hand vigorously. "Thank you so much," he said. And he walked through the

70

Victorian doors of the piano bar, contemplating a young Jew
hearing of the death camps from a survivor.

The next week Joseph went to pick up his son from school
for a doctor's appointment. Derrick's class was playing in the
tree park across the way. He stood a long while and watched
as the children hurtled about in all different directions. They
were all part of a beautiful chaos of jumping, skipping,
springing, delirious laughter. It was as if someone had
opened a chest of living, animated gems that had burst out
and were swirling about the playground. They rolled in the
grass and pounded the ground with their feet. Then they
stopped suddenly and sprung into the air, one jumping as
high as he could, the others following, bouncing high in
mimicry, then abandoning this game with fickle spite and
charging like sprites to a new interest at the opposite end of
the ground.

Dizzy from watching their mini-orbits, Joseph looked
away and judged his life. Since his youth he had been
obsessed with freedom and spritely wanderlust. He didn't
want to change. He was drunk with the flutter of wasp's
wings, with the fine sap of open space. But now he looked on
these feelings as if they were objects. He looked coldly, skep-
tically on his cherished memories.

He turned back to the children. In the center of them was
his own boy Derrick, the wildest of the infant mob, running,
stopping, turning, rising on his heels, and shrieking with
laughter. Joseph felt a wondrous swell. His body flushed with

love as he called out. Derrick turned, saw him, and shouted, his voice ringing with gladness. Then he pointed passionately at the clouds.

Hi, Daddy!

Look up in the sky.

VIRGIN

Joseph and Caleb were hardly dream lovers, but they felt sweetly for each other. In a year together they had teased and frustrated each other; shared a fiery, fractious love; and schemed emotionally, playing their respective trump cards as younger boy and older man. In between all this they found their moments of tender intimacy. Caleb even believed he could read his lover's mind from miles away, at night alone in his bedroom in Brooklyn.

They first met on a magically sunny day. Indian summer was in its high, late fury, chasing Joseph out of doors and downtown to Greenwich Village. There he stood on the corner of Sheridan Square, admiring the shirtless boys clapping their hands and laughing outrageously in the street. It was blazing on the corner; the white sidewalks were radiant. Parched and bored, Joseph was about to cross the street for a drink in the rawhide bar when his eyes fell on a long-legged teen in a baseball cap walking briskly east.

Love muffin! was his first thought. *Can't let him get away.*

The wispy youth was nicely dressed — well taken care of, Joseph thought — and something about him suggested emotional frailty. Besides his Yankee cap he wore a white tennis shirt and tight blue shorts that creased his small butt halves into the shape of balloons. And what legs! Long, built for easy bending. Curved like a stream of pouring water. Formidable weapons in any war of lust.

Hurrying along, he seemed embarrassed in his tiny short pants, as if afraid that hungry men were watching him from behind the coal-tinted window in the rawhide bar. Joseph turned on his heel and darted after him — there wasn't time to be subtle. Caleb glanced over his shoulder, kept walking, and looked again after half a block.

Joseph caught up to him seated by the chess tables in Washington Square Park. He came and sat nearby, terribly curious about this long-legged boy who liked baseball *and* chess. *Nice butt* and *a brain?* he wondered. Caleb saw him staring and frowned. The boy might even have insulted him, Joseph wasn't sure, when he whispered into a friend's ear and laughed harshly.

Put off, Joseph left, but he returned the next afternoon. Caleb was in the park again, in long pants this time, setting up his black and white wooden knights and pawns. Again he looked at Joseph, but today he didn't frown.

"You want to play?" he asked.

"Okay," Joseph said warily, being barely a novice at chess.

"I play for money."

"Okay. Let's play for a quarter."

A junior chess master, Caleb gingerly played with his lover-to-be, passing up several chances to checkmate, both to extend their game and as a first show of tenderness. He even moved his pieces with affection. At last he couldn't help but trap Joseph's king, queen, and rook in one move. He leaned back on the park bench and lit a cigarette.

"You stink," he said.

"Oh, you're a wise guy, huh?"

"Nope. I'm not wise." Caleb smiled.

"There's more important things in life than chess," said Joseph. "Painting. Art. Politics. School."

"Chess *is* life. And school is bullshit."

Joseph conceded the teenage point of view. He decided to start over.

"It's beautiful in this park in summer. The musicians. People playing ball. Lovers holding hands."

Caleb's smile changed fluidly into a small frown. A woman walked by pushing a baby in a stroller. Then a young girl playing with her lively red setter. There was a sparkle of sadness in Caleb's eyes. "I'm having a bad day," he said, bafflingly.

Joseph felt a flash of excitement. Already he felt emotionally locked to the boy. "Anyway, you're not supposed to tell people they stink," he teased. "Didn't your parents teach you manners?"

Caleb giggled. "I was just being honest."

"Well, this time I'm whipping your butt," said Joseph. "Set up the board."

This is how they got along at first. Caleb won again, Joseph vowed revenge, and they played game after game through the hot Indian summer afternoon.

In the following weeks Joseph looked for Caleb in the park almost every day. They played chess and poker for quarters, teasing each other happily. Other chess experts, older than Caleb, sometimes came by to challenge him, and Joseph watched and rooted him on. "You're brilliant," Joe said when Caleb won. When he lost, Joseph petulantly cursed the winner. "He can't get it up," he'd grumble. "I saw him eating a dead cat down on the Bowery." As Caleb laughed, Joseph leaned close to whisper playful malevolence in his ear, not remembering that he had learned this game years ago from his ten-year-old son.

It wasn't clear that Caleb liked men, but there were hints. When he went to the deli for an orange seltzer, he'd bring back an extra for Joseph. He even let Joseph win a chess game or two. Soon Joseph could feel his fresh, aroused gaze. If Joseph wandered away from the tables or spoke to another man, he would turn to catch Caleb watching him intently.

He's infatuated with me, thought Joseph. And this was true. Caleb had fallen in love with him, suddenly and inexplicably, as often happens.

The boy had an inflaming impact on the man. Though some days he could look rather plain — bloated and pale after a night of hard teenage drinking. But on most days Caleb was beautiful. His mouth was small and dreamlike.

There was a tiny, voluptuous curve under the bridge of his nose. His face had an angular cut that gave his loveliness momentum — classic square-jawed handsomeness compressed onto a narrow beam. As a prism changes colors in turning light, he seemed to change from day to day. Some days spare, almost sickly; some days rangy and robust. Sunnily content, then harsh and miserable. Boyish when he sat with his legs spread wide, inviting oral sex. Girlish when he crossed his legs and held a cigarette with his wrist flung back, his wide eyes begging a bull-brained forward charge.

Joseph caught himself breathing shallowly. *He is young. So was Macon, though,* he thought. But Caleb was a virgin, with men at least. Looking into the childish blue eyes, Joseph was sure of it.

But how could anyone seduce him so completely without trying? Why spread his crotch canyonwide, fraying the denim seam, for Joe to see? Why, near sundown, tired from the sun, did he glower open-mouthed at passing men? There was a fair enough chance the boy meant business. A fair enough chance to take.

And if Joseph didn't have him, some other man would. Someone else would get him in bed, fill him with lies and sperm, and leave death behind, swimming asleep in his baby blood. Caleb was across the way as Joseph pondered, talking with a man who sold marijuana in the park.

The bastard will kill him, Joseph thought, peering at the bald, eroded man who now had his hand on Caleb's shoulder.

Joseph lowered his head. Then he looked up, his mind's eye flashing white with hostility — *Take your goddamn hands off my lover* — toward the scar-faced dealer, who was leading Caleb toward his drug stash hidden in the bushes. He decided not to wait another day.

Can I talk to you, Caleb?
No, you can't, you damn queer!
"Can I talk to you, Caleb?"
"Sure, Joe. What do you say?"

He invited him to a baseball game, stammering as he asked, still worried he was doing something wrong. But Caleb grinned broadly as he inspected the tickets.

"Third-row seats to the Yankees? Are you kidding?" He gave Joseph a shove. "Of course I'll go."

"Next Saturday then?" Joseph mirrored the teenager's bright smile with his own.

"Definitely."

At the stadium they cheered at pop flies and double plays and slapped high fives when the Yanks scored. Caleb sat with his shoes up on his seat, guzzling beer and eating popcorn. Periodically he gave raspberries to the umpire. Screaming after an "atrocious call," he choked on a corn kernel, and Joseph smacked him on the back. "Thanks, bub," he said after his throat cleared, his eyes darting erotically.

The Yankee cleanup batter was a tall man with a bull's behind and a face full of menacing, wiry hair. Caleb knew everything about the all-star, his batting statistics and even personal data. ("You should see his wife. She's a fox.") When the slugger smashed a home run over the left-field wall, Caleb jumped in his seat, spilling beer into his lap and tossing popcorn into the air. The stadium erupted with noise, thousands in unison chanting the cleanup batter's name. Joseph smiled as his young escort had to wipe tears from his eyes.

The home run was the highlight of the game. Through the last three innings, Joseph and Caleb sat with their knees touching and their elbows sharing the armrest, scanning the crowd for banners. There was one last roar of cheers as the Yankee pitcher left the game. Caleb began to shiver as the sun dropped below the stadium wall.

"You're getting cold?" asked Joseph.

"My pants are wet." Joseph helped him sop the cold beer out of his pants with paper towels. "My dick is gonna get drunk," Caleb muttered.

After the game they went for a drive, past smoking factory towers and railcar lots along the Harlem River, over the bridge and past the teeming junk barges in the bay. They drove the far way around Manhattan, then up along the West Street waterfront. They stopped at an Italian restaurant near Joseph's home and shared a pizza. Caleb didn't say much, his mouth stuffed all the while with tomatoes. Joseph made small talk about the game and about the neighborhood. He felt hesitant, almost afraid. At last he spoke his mind.

"You want to come to my apartment for a drink?"

Caleb stopped chewing. He put down his pizza and blinked, then haltingly agreed. Joseph smiled doubtfully as the expression on Caleb's face turned gray and somber by increments.

They sat on Joseph's bed sipping Grand Marnier. Caleb looked around the bedroom. There were magazines, pictures of men on the wall.

"Tell the truth, Joe. Are you gay?"

"Yes!"

Caleb moved away on the bed. "I didn't know," he stuttered.

"Yes, you did."

"Really, I didn't."

"Yes, you did."

"Being gay is all right."

"Thank you," Joseph said ironically.

Caleb cocked his head thoughtfully. "You can't tell to look at you."

Joseph straightened the sheets behind him. "You mean I don't act like a sissy?"

The boy's eyes flickered and searched the wall.

"That's only a stereotype," Joseph continued. "People used to say black men had tails. White people actually believed it."

"They were jerks," said Caleb.

"What I'm saying is that it's just another kind of prejudice. I'm proud I'm gay. It's beautiful."

"I have a friend who's lesbian."

"Good for you."

A juvenile smile flickered on Caleb's face and then dissolved into a frightened expression. Joseph held his gaze, inspecting the quivering folds around his mouth.

"Did you know you were going to invite me here after the ball game?" he asked.

"I thought about it."

"But you didn't try to hide — you know, those sex magazines and stuff."

Joseph dropped his hand to his pants zipper.

"I always try to be honest."

"That's impressive." Caleb drained his glass of liquor and lifted his knee sensually up onto the bed. His manner now was ever-so-slightly girlish. "Do you have a boyfriend?"

"No, but I did. Sort of." Joseph told him about Macon — how they met, about all the terrible trouble. The story of sordid street danger fascinated Caleb.

"Now I want a new boyfriend." Joseph spoke deliberately in a deep, warm voice. "Someone handsome, smart, and adorable. Like you, for instance."

Caleb scowled horribly.

"That is, if you were gay."

Caleb stood up and wandered around the bedroom, picking up and inspecting trinkets: poker chips, a cheap plastic ring. He stopped before a photograph of Derrick on the bureau. Derrick was fifteen in the picture.

"You know, my dad used to take me to Yankee games."

That's why the hat! inferred Joseph.

Caleb stood now at a framed photograph on the wall of a muscled model in a leather T-shirt.

"Do you like that picture?" asked Joseph.

Caleb turned nervously. For an instant he seemed to get very angry. Then he calmed but still didn't speak.

"Are you okay?"

He just stood with his hands in his pockets. "I better be going, Joe," he said finally. And he left.

But he came back a week later. Again they sat on the bed, sipping liquor. Caleb was relaxed and visibly excited. Resting on the bed in bare feet and sweatpants, Joseph decided to relax as well — and wait. His visitor was in the mood to talk.

And talk he did, for the longest while. About his young life mostly, while Joseph listened with furious, precise attention. Dirtying the sheets with his sneaker heels, Caleb lied ridiculously about his sex life. "Girls love it when I *fuck* them!" he nearly shouted. He avoided the subject of school. He talked about his father — about their family vacation in Israel, about his father's recent heart trouble, how his father had divorced his mother and remarried and was now separated from his second wife.

Rolling onto his side, Caleb stretched out his arms like a kitten. An erection pushed about visibly in his jeans. "I had a bad experience once," he said. And he told of how, when he was fifteen, a strange man followed him from a subway train, approached him on the platform, and frightened him.

Is he telling the whole truth? Joseph wondered. He could guess why the man had followed. The eyes were dead giveaways, as bright and alarming as beacons.

Caleb was looking at him now, plaintively. Joseph drummed his fingers on Caleb's kneecap. He pinched a bit of denim. Caught in a pocket, his penis snapped across his thigh inside his sweatpants. Startled, Caleb leapt up from the bed, knocking pillows onto the floor. He apologized, straightened up the bed, then politely sat back down, closer.

Joseph fondly scratched the small of his back, all the while gazing upon ethereal details of Caleb's features. The fallen cheeks, the blond hair thin as fibers. Most of all the blue war-orphan sadness of his eyes.

He expected a last-minute protest. But Caleb kicked off his sneakers and lay back against the pillows. Beneath his zipper, his nightlong erection breathed.

"What's up, Joe?" he whispered.

Joseph pulled off Caleb's cotton sweater. Hastily, off came his wrinkled jeans. Then the apple-red Jockey shorts, hooked for a moment over the tip of his penis, now twitching stiff. Joseph pulled down his sweatpants and lay comfortably on top of the entirely nude boy.

He felt as if he were lying facedown in a running stream of hot water. He could taste hot water splashing in his mouth, rolling over the back of his neck. But there was no water, only the warmth of the palpably gullible youth beneath him.

Joseph sucked in his breath so quickly that it dried and burned his tongue.

"Just this once," he whispered.

It was evil. (It was so fucking easy.) It was wrong. But judgment made no difference. It was sex that danced in Joseph's mind like a headless puppet. Caleb lifted his legs, his rump served up with inflaming prominence. Such virgin instinct! — to naturally assume the loveliest, most whorish pose he could have. Wincing, Joseph pressed into the dough-soft bottom. It was tight. There, it slipped a bit. He glanced up and saw that Caleb looked afraid.

"Relax."

Caleb smiled unconvincingly.

"I *have* to," Joseph said. "You understand?"

"Yes."

"Your ass is a miracle, you hear me?" Joseph said.

"I hear you."

After long minutes of whispered encouragement, the softness began to give. Joseph locked his hips to hold the spot.

"Ouch!"

"What's wrong?"

"It pinches."

"Good. It's good when it hurts. Right?"

The boy's eyes went dead. "Right."

Minutes passed. Caleb's fingers grasped in finicky snatches at the sheets. Joseph was in past the change in color of his prick. Enough to begin fucking the teenager by the inch, then an inch and a half. Two inches. Three. Four. Five. Six...

I have him.

Whimpers came from below. Grunts and squeals. The sex noise swirled like smoke into Joseph's ears, accelerated and searched like a starved reptile for the base of his brain, found it, and bit down hard. The sound ran along his nerves to the center of his mind and, once there, reveled, like horses burning in a barn. Bad horses, evil men. Bad men — murderers — had broken into Joseph's mind, as into a house, and were smashing the furniture, breaking glass, torching the walls, and laughing.

Around him, legs flounced like the arms of a gesticulating puppet. Feet climbed up his chest and groped for a place on his shoulders. Together they found the perfect spot, in a corner, buried in linen and sweaty down.

There was a gasp of surprise. Joseph felt as if he were being swallowed whole.

I've got it. I've got it.

His hips bolted quickly. It wouldn't be long, he knew. "First piece of cock," he growled witlessly. "Beautiful...virgin ass." A narrow electric beam ran down the center of his penis. It had turned on; it was flashing light. The beam was firing. Joseph stopped moving and came with a vicious, lingering sweetness. He shuddered, stiffened for a moment, then pulled away.

Immediately he felt guilty. Sadistic, gluttonous. To relieve the guilt he needed to be tender. He traced a circle on the boy's stomach, rubbed his fingers on the damp flesh under his testicles. Then he let the birdlike legs fall from his shoulders to the bed. Caleb stared at the wall, holding his breath.

"That was good," said Caleb vacantly as though he were alone in the room. Joseph stood up and went into the bathroom to wash his hands and face.

As the cold water ran, he avoided looking in the mirror.

He came back and stood in the doorway, silhouetted against the bathroom light. Caleb lay quietly, playing with his penis. Joseph realized he hadn't come, that he might be disappointed but too shy to ask. *I'll do him in a minute,* Joseph thought. He had to catch his breath first. And savor and ponder what had just happened.

He wanted to shout his triumph. Cherry! Cherry! But he knew the risk he had taken was murderous and wrong. Still, it was wonderful, like alchemy — a boy transformed into a girl, a lie into the truth, a virgin into a sopping slut. And he had given of himself. For all of his life, Caleb would remember the past few minutes in Joseph's bed. Hopefully his life would be a long one.

I can't do that again, Joseph thought. He looked fondly down at Caleb, at his soft, girlish hips and at his beckoning penis. Then Joseph moved to the bed and tended to his boyhood.

The next week they were together again. After a drink and a cigarette, Caleb put his arms around Joseph and kissed him. Joseph was pleased. The kid seemed eager and confident.

"Joey, let's do what we did last time."

A patch of hair flashed in candlelight as Caleb threw his legs over his head, kicking like a colt out of his gray jeans.

"Show me again," said Joseph.

Grinning, Caleb threw back his legs, trapped his thighs in his hands and playfully showed again the wispy patch of golden hair in the middle of his butt.

Now Joseph understood. It was the bending and kicking. The tuft of hair, like golden farmer's hay. And inside, like farmer's soil — *the pitchfork, the rake* — like moist, black earth. He could forgive himself a single lapse in safety. He would never do it again. But his desire was brilliantly awakened now, pulling like a divining rod tuned to treasure.

"Caleb, we have to use these." He opened the night-table drawer and pulled out a box of condoms.

"Okay," Caleb said, eyeing the package with almost solemn interest, as if he were in school.

It didn't work that night. Fumbling, Joseph turned the damn thing inside out. In frustration he lost his erection. Trying again with another, he frothed and spilled on Caleb's stomach.

For a while they were happy with just French kisses and sleeping in each other's arms. But eventually they mastered the lifesaving technique. Caleb was patient, forgiving when his lover failed. But Joseph felt exposed, even disembodied, while Caleb figured the damn thing out, glancing back and forth with savage eagerness between Joseph and the rubber.

Caleb discovered a quirk in his lover — anytime he wanted, he could make him hard by rubbing his feet in the old guy's face. No matter if he was bare or in clean sweat socks, it always worked. Caleb slipped on the condom, having become quite nimble with it. Then he lay back, lifted his legs, and played on Joseph's face with the cold, soft soles of his feet. Joseph would rise infallibly, like a tollgate.

Joseph didn't care to analyze the symbolism of his reflex hard-on. And Caleb treated it so matter of factly. He made no innuendo, never slyly grinned. But it seemed to Joseph that the kid was now in control of their sex.

He can't be that innocent, Joseph thought. *That bunny-rabbit routine. He's using his ass, his pubic hair, and his long legs and stocking feet to take control of me.*

And it's working. I love him so much.

And this was true. Joseph had fallen, as if from a tall cliff, utterly in love with Caleb. It might have been the sex, the touching, the all-night mutual confessions. It could have been his talent for chess and the piano. Or his voice that warbled with anxiety. Or the deep well of hurt that Joseph was just now detecting.

And, yes, it was the class, the boy's breeding. Joseph found him exotic, this young, well-born Jew whose mother could pay for chess lessons from an Israeli grand master. Caleb's Jewishness was lovely erotic spice. Music in the voice. Fine gestures and echoes of family. It made a difference. Joseph would happily fuck the enemy, suck off the enemy, French-kiss the enemy, but could he ever love — desperately *love* — the distant son of a Christian slave owner or a British colonialist?

Jews had traded slaves, he thought. But it had taken a historian to uncover that. That bit of history didn't buzz in your ears like the legacy of the English. It wasn't part of the blanket of public stupidity that embraced nearly everyone in the city, the ridiculous subtext of public life on the streets. Joseph hated the unspoken communication between strangers on the city sidewalk: I'm blond. I'm white. I make more money. You have a bigger dick. I wear a suit and tie. You take it in the ass. I drive a better car. You've been to prison. I have cable television. You have a VCR? Well, they've come down in price. I come from the Ivy League. You're a suspect. The cops are on my side. I rule the world. You used to be a slave. Technology. Riot. I'm better. You resent me. Size doesn't count. You wish you had a white woman. Money isn't happiness.

It's okay to love a Jewish boy, he decided.

But regardless of whatever he might have decided, Joseph was in love with Caleb. He was…inflamed by his androgyny, dazzled by his prime colors, flattered by his shyness. And the war-orphan pathos! He always wanted to see him. His voice leapt out of his throat when the boy called on the telephone. "Hi, Caleb!" He gave up pretending to be casual.

And by himself he schemed to make the love deeper, even obsessive, if he could. *How can I make him obsessed with me?* he asked. Then he remembered. *My father used to take me to baseball games.*

93

There's the window, thought Joseph. And like a reckless burglar, he sneaked through it.

It was warm, shimmering magic when Joseph wrapped his arms and legs around Caleb's small, radiating body. He felt as if he were nursing an infant, and the love flowed out from him as a mother's milk must flow from full, dripping breasts.

In the mornings, after breakfast, they went for drives or took long walks. For years before, Joe had made plans to entertain his lover when he finally had one. When he was in Providence, Victor Quincy told him stories of long walks to secret, magical places his lover had sought out especially for him. "There was a wooden bridge over a stream in Brockton," said Victor. "The water sounded like a chorus of flutes. And there was this bakery on Beacon Hill." In New York, Joseph made note of all the special places he could find. The most imaginative shops or the strangest. Charming alcoves that seemed out of another time in history. Side streets that cast their own peculiar spell. He dreamed of taking walks and showing such places, like gifts, to his lover one day.

It was on such a walk in the nooks and crannies of Greenwich Village, down by the truck depots where New York changed magically into a small town, that they met Julio one Sunday afternoon. He was standing idly with a foot against the wall, in biker's shorts, his bent knee looking like a golden fruit, his skin like almond cake frosting. He was about nineteen. He touched Caleb and made him laugh; he paid not much attention to Joseph. But when he grabbed his crotch, Joseph's blood performed a fire dance. Joseph wanted to be had by Julio — it had been an eternity — though not actually, and besides it was obvious that Julio wanted Caleb. They talked about music. Joking and posing, Julio was still busy with his balls and cock. Idly touching, brutally tugging, sculpting the shape in his shorts. Scratching furiously, searching underneath. Joseph and Caleb both were captive, dumbstruck by the show.

It frightened Joseph, what Julio could do to his sparrowlike lover. Yet he wanted it to happen. If he couldn't give himself to Julio, then he would give him Caleb. Golden Julio, with his temperamental crotch, his long lashes ringing walnut-brown eyes, and his fruitlike knees! *He should have what he wants,* Joseph decided.

"I have to run," he said suddenly.

"Run where?" asked Caleb, staring confusedly as Julio put an arm around his waist.

"I'll call you later."

Joseph walked off and left them. As he drove back home, he saw in his mind what was happening back at the truck stop. Caleb with his jeans around his ankles, hidden between two diesel trucks. Julio with one leg up on a standpipe. Caleb with one foot dangling out of a trailer.

Once home Joseph masturbated to violent images of Julio and his fragile lover.

Caleb never mentioned Julio. To Joseph this was proof that something had happened. Though possibly Caleb had simply gone home from the truck stop and forgot everything.

No, Joseph was certain they had kissed all afternoon, fucked in a big white bed all night, and exchanged telephone numbers and had been together since. He frowned at Caleb impenetrably, so irrationally jealous that he felt exhausted.

Derrick had sent him a photograph in his track suit holding a statewide trophy. Joseph framed the photograph and put it on the coffee table. The next time Caleb came to visit, he pointed the photo out.

"Isn't he handsome? He won this in the Ohio State unilaterals."

Caleb looked, shrugged, and said nothing.

"And he's doing well in school."

Caleb lit a cigarette, leaned back, and turned on the television.

"He's a good athlete. I was a good runner when I was his age. Your age, you know. I won a lot of races. But I never won statewide."

"You got any liquor here, Joe?"

"There's some scotch in the kitchen."

Caleb bounded up, wiggled his hips and smiled, and went into the kitchen. He came back with two drinks, for himself and Joseph, who was still looking at the photograph.

"He's a good son. He makes me very happy."

Caleb sipped his scotch and faked a burp. Then he took a long drag on his cigarette. He stared blankly, tiredly at the television screen.

"This show sucks," he said quietly.

Caleb had planned to leave after dinner, but he decided at the last moment to stay the night. He helped Joseph wash the dishes. About midnight they went to bed and made love. Caleb was beggingly open, almost abject, his bottom greedy as a suckling. When they kissed, his lips seemed to melt. He became like a warm liquid, a hot primordial pool. Joseph felt as if he were bathing in boy.

Afterward, while Caleb slept, Joseph remained awake, confused, hurt, satisfied, disgusted with himself. The wind blew the curtains up, and Caleb's face was illuminated in starlight. He appeared to wear a mask of whiteness. To Joseph the color of his lover's skin looked arbitrary, accidental, and unreal.

It was 2, 3, 4 o'clock in the morning. Caleb sat on the bed with his head against Joseph's shoulder, complaining about his father.

"He smokes like a steamboat. He won't stop. My mom yells at him when she visits, but he still smokes. He's gonna have another heart attack. It scares me."

"Calm down, baby."

Caleb was smoking himself at the time. He took a long look at his cigarette — he imagined it was a dead penis. Then he looked at Joe. "I'm going to die of cancer. I know it. That doesn't scare me."

"You're breaking my heart, Cal."

"Can't you tell I'm tense? I'm always worried about my dad, even when I'm not thinking about him."

"Your father could live another twenty years." Joe tickled Caleb's ear as he said this, squeezing the soft cartilage, the part that feels like a bird's bone.

"It's just that he's *old*. I know his time is not limitless."

"It won't be as bad as you think."

Caleb rolled over and rested his head in Joseph's lap. "What was it like when your father died, Joe?"

Joseph had memorized the details of his father's funeral, for even at fifteen he thought he might paint the scene one day. The light-skinned choir leader with short red hair and white pearl earrings. Her satin white robe with a purple-and-gold band down the middle and wide pink cuffs. Her arms raised, her head thrown back as she sang, "So much joy, so much gladness, so much happiness." Passionately exhaling the *s*'s as if she were exhaling evil from her soul. The preacher shouted, "Where is this? This is heaven? Those are God's angels. Their robes have been washed in the blood of the lamb."

"That's a cool image," said Caleb. "A white robe washed in lamb's blood."

"Yeah, it is cool."

"What else?" Caleb asked.

"My Aunt Jessie. A full, hot-blooded Baptist. She got on her knees and clapped, screaming 'Hallelujah!' over and over."

"Thank you, Jesus," Caleb said.

"You got it," said Joe.

Caleb got up on his knees on the bed. "Thank you, Je-sus! Thank you Jee-sus!" Joe laughed.

Caleb quieted down again. "You like it when I act dopey, don't you?"

Joseph winced.

"Did you cry?"

"I cried and cried," said Joey. He didn't seem very sad right then. "I don't know where all the tears came from."

Caleb thought for a long moment, wondering if he would cry when the day came. *What about Joe's son?* he wondered. *Would Derrick cry if his faggot father died?*

"Why don't you get tested, Joe?"

"I'm afraid to."

"Don't be afraid. I'd bet my life you're negative."

"Why?"

"Because I'm negative." Caleb had taken the test last winter, months after he and Joe first fucked skin on skin.

Joe's eyebrows shaded over. "It doesn't work like that."

Caleb crawled into Joe's lap and rocked his butt there slowly, the way he liked.

"Am I your best boyfriend ever?"

"Yes."

"I'm better than Macon was?"

"You're the best." Joseph snapped at Caleb's earlobe as if he were shooting marbles.

"Macon," Caleb said. He was talking queenily now. "That cheap prostitute. I bet he walks down Tenth Avenue and picks up used condoms on the street and sucks them clean for breakfast."

"That's disgusting."

"He's a crack fiend, Joe." Caleb knew he was being a hypocrite, since he'd done some drugs himself. "I don't know why you miss him."

Joseph was silent.

"What's wrong?"

"Nothing," said Joe.

Caleb reached for his wallet. "Want to see a picture of my baby brother? This is my mom's baby from her new husband. Six months."

"Yes, he's very beautiful," said Joseph.

Caleb was dissatisfied that Joseph seemed unhappy. To please him he did a sex trick he had proudly invented. "Giving a face job," he called it. He rubbed his face around and around in the crotch of Joseph's shorts (or sometimes when Joe was naked). Mostly he used his nose, but he put his cheeks and eyes in there too. He rubbed and pressed and nuzzled. Up and down, side to side. Rolling his face in a circle under warm testicles.

"Stop it!" Joe cried.

"I thought you liked it."

"I don't want to mess up my clean shorts." But Joseph sat up smiling and hunched up his shoulders as he did when he was relaxed.

Caleb was glad he had made him feel better. He went into the kitchen and brought back two glasses of ice water. They kissed for a long while. Later as Joseph slept, Caleb thought about Julio. And he thought about his vanished rival, Macon, whom he knew only through Joseph's stories. As much as Joe loved Caleb, Macon had touched him in a place he had not. Caleb knew this. *I'm a real jealous kid,* he thought to himself.

SONS AND LOVERS

"Dad, tell me the truth. Are you gay?"

Derrick was stretching in just his jockstrap in front of the hall mirror. His father had gone out. He was barely aware that he was talking aloud.

"I saw two *guys* holding hands today, Dad. What do you think of that?"

He peered into the mirror at the contrast of the white jockstrap against his dark skin, then at the whitish-pink color of his palms. He lifted the back of his hand to his mouth and sucked on oak-brown flesh.

"Fuck it," he said. He dropped to the floor and did a flurry of push-ups, then rolled over on his back and lay still. After a moment he leapt to his feet.

"So, Dad, where's your girlfriend?" He was shadowboxing now, throwing strong, wild uppercuts into the air.

"Damn, I'm talking to myself."

He lay down on the sofa, picked up the telephone, and dialed the number of his longtime friend Toast. The phone

rang several times before a coarse, sleepy voice finally
answered.

"Who the *fuck* is it?"

"Your mother's worst nightmare, chump."

"Yo, Chiller. When you get back, man?"

"A week ago. I been hanging with my Pops."

"When you coming out to Brooklyn, man?"

"Soon, very soon." Derrick chatted with his friend for a
brief while and then hung up and called his grandmother.

"Hi, Grandma Grace."

"Is that you, Derrick? Your father said you were back in
town."

"Whazzup?"

"I'm fine. Your voice is so deep, child. You sound just like
the man on television."

"I just called to say hello."

"When you coming to see me?"

"Very soon. Tomorrow. I'm hanging up now, okay?"

Next Derrick called his girlfriend long-distance in
Cincinnati. They shared several minutes of teenage love chat-
ter, silly and private in its meaning. Derrick told Wanda he
would call again next week and abruptly hung up the receiver.

He picked up a tattered copy of *The Autobiography of
Malcolm X* from the coffee table. Turning to a dog-eared
page, he read a few familiar words and tossed the book back.

He bounded up from the sofa and searched around the living room for anything of interest. On his father's desk he
found a leather datebook. Flipping through the pages, he

came upon a telephone number for Caleb Zive. "That's that white devil with the mouth," he said aloud. He scratched his eyebrow a long moment, then wrote the number on a scrap of paper and stuffed it into his jock.

He lay back down on the sofa. "I have gay blood," he said dreamily. He sat up suddenly. "Is it hereditary? Am I going to turn homo?"

Curious at the prospect, Derrick used a technique he learned in yoga class. He began visualizing men to test whether or not they aroused him. In his mind he saw the Cincinnati Reds cleanup slugger swinging for the fence, his favorite movie star getting the girl. "Nope. I don't feel it." He squeezed his eyelids shut, trying to detect the faintest bit of desire. Mr. Universe. The welterweight champ. The tough guy on the cop show. Nothing. He opened his eyes.

"Nope. I love vagina, baby."

And this was true. Derrick loved the feminine genital gift. It was maddeningly soft, salty, pink, and mushy. "And it stinks!" His favorite thing was to bury his nose in vulva, the mushroomy musk rushing his brain like a narcotic. He imagined a Rastaman puffing hashish, eyeballs rolling in delight. Derrick liked to laugh in bed. He liked to be creative. Diagonal strokes, then widening circles, then slow. *Slow,* baby, like ladling soup. Never the same way twice.

Derrick had aroused himself uncomfortably. He gripped the fabric of his jockstrap and stretched it to make extra room. Then he sank deep into the corner of the sofa, picked up the phone, and called Cincinnati again.

"What's wrong with you, Derrick?" exclaimed Wanda when she heard his voice.

"Nothing, girl."

"But you just called me not five minutes ago. And you practically hung up on me."

"Listen, Wanda. Guess what I'm wearing."

"Don't tell me you're naked, Derrick."

"No, I'm not naked. I'm almost naked."

"And you just had to call to tell me that?"

Before slamming down the receiver, Wanda told him he was silly and nasty and not to call her again unless he was wearing clothes.

He sat on the sofa for a long while in silence, his eyes drifting about the living room, coming to rest on the compact disc player. The Red Hot Chili Peppers. What did Caleb say to him in the office? Something about his color. He wanted to slap him right there. Tiny parts of his muscles had already started in motion when he decided, *Not in front of my father.*

But out in the street, he wouldn't have hesitated. Pop! in the face and kept on walking. Like that time in the Cincinnati suburbs. *What you doing in this neighborhood, Bosco?* Pop! pop! and he was blocks away before the police could have known.

Derrick flinched as he realized he was digging into his cheek with his fingernail. "Fuck this shit," he burst out.

He walked over to the stereo system and hurriedly disconnected the plugs to his father's compact disc player. Then he carried it out onto the terrace. He looked below.

There were Dumpsters and janitor's equipment on the ground level. No one was in sight, either below or on any neighboring terrace.

He rested the player on the terrace wall, steadying it with his elbow as he gazed out past the surrounding buildings to the Hudson River. Though his heart was beating hard, he felt calm. He looked down again. Then he shoved the CD player over, following it with his eyes as it twirled cartwheels in the air all the way down and crashed into pieces on the ground below.

"Damn," he said.

He closed the terrace door behind him, pulled off his jock, and lay down on the living room rug.

He rolled over and stared at the Arabian horses sewn into the red and gold carpet. He remembered lying on this rug when he was eleven years old, brushing his fingers over the shiny manes of the handwoven upright stallions, cupping his chin in the thinker's pose and speculating about his dad, asleep on the floor so close that Derrick felt the warmth of his body. That was the summer the boats came, the Navy flotilla firing cannon over the harbor to celebrate Liberty. They had barbecued and watched the fireworks show from the terrace. Stuffing themselves with steak, washing it down with cold juice, they gazed up at explosions that bathed their faces in blue, red, and white light. Both of them ate too much; they had to digest the barbecue lying down on the carpet.

"You eat like a moose," Derrick teased.

His father tickled his stomach. Then, just before falling asleep, he told Derrick a lie. "I'm going to talk to your mother. You're going to come live with me again. Very soon."

It never happened. It was a good lie that turned cruel. Perhaps his father was trying to make up for that other lie or what sounded like a lie to Derrick. "We're all human first, black and white, all the same in our hearts." So instead of punching the white boy who touched him out on Coney Island, he made a friend who would live for only months. But after the boy's family barred Derrick from setting one black foot in the funeral home, he was sure his father had lied. He felt it again now, bigotry and grief double-helixed into a screw, then screwed into his heart — his father was *wrong*.

And his father knew it and had loved him as hard as he could for the rest of the summer of Liberty. Loved him enough to lie again. A good lie; this one felt so warm until it died and turned cold and cruel.

Derrick laughed lightly to remember. He was ashamed to admit how much it hurt that his father's promise never came true, how until only recently he had yet expected that it would.

He drifted off and might have slept for a minute or an hour, waking up to the jangle of keys unlocking the front door. "Dad!" he exclaimed under his breath, remembering he was nude. He jumped up from the rug and ran into the bathroom to dress.

When he came out, his father was in the middle of the living room with his palm pressed to his forehead. He seemed preoccupied.

"Where you been?" asked Derrick.

"Oh, hi, buddy. I was at the office doing the payroll with Douglas."

"Did you talk to that devil?"

"What?"

Derrick went into the kitchen and came back with a bottle of spring water.

"Does Caleb do any work? He just hangs around and gets paid?"

"Of course he works."

"You should give jobs to black brothers, Dad. Not to blue-eyed devils."

"Last time I looked Dolores was black."

Derrick took a swig of water. "I think Caleb is gay."

"What makes you say that?"

"He looks at me funny."

There was a long silence. "It's your imagination," Joseph said finally.

"No," Derrick persisted. "He's gay all right. What do you think?"

"I think you need to mind your business."

"Forget it," answered Derrick, trying to sound curt.

"You know, you're not going to sit around on your butt all summer! I want you to learn — where's my CD player?"

"Oh, yeah. I had a little accident."

"Please don't tell me you broke it."

"I dropped it off the terrace."

"What?"

"I'll pay for it, all right. I don't want to talk about it."

111

"You what? What?"

"I said I'll pay for it!"

"Off the terrace? What?"

"Dad, I want to go stay with Grandma Grace in Brooklyn."

Joseph fumbled the papers he was holding, then dropped them to the floor.

"Of course. You always spend a little time there when you visit."

"No, I want to go today. No, tomorrow."

"Well, I've made a lot of plans. I bought tickets—" He bent over to pick up his papers.

Derrick was silent.

"But you want to go to Brooklyn."

"Yes."

"For a few days?"

"'Til I go back to Cincinnati."

A moment passed before Joseph could speak.

"If that's what you want," he said finally.

The next morning Joseph and Derrick drove over the Manhattan Bridge and through the cobbled streets of Brooklyn. Derrick's bags were in the backseat.

"Hoo, baby! Look at those titties. Pop, check out the females."

Joseph stared straight ahead, cursing at the traffic.

"Look, Pop! It's Miss Black America." Derrick stuck his head out the car window. "Hey, baby, it's Love Man. Love Man, sister!"

A doubled-parked truck stopped their progress. Derrick pulled his head in and rolled up the window.

"You get along good with white people, don't you?" he asked.

"I try to get along with everybody, Derrick."

"You ever read *The Autobiography of Malcolm X*?"

"Of course. You don't understand Malcolm."

Derrick sucked his teeth. *You suck the white man's dick and try to tell me.*

"You should read 'Letter to My Nephew' by James Baldwin."

"James Baldwin. Ain't he a faggot?"

Joseph squinted terribly, a curse caught in his throat. The stoplight turned red, and two men in denim cutoffs crossed the street.

"Look at that. I bet those guys are gay." Derrick rolled down his window. "Homos!" he shouted.

"Shut the hell up, Derrick, all right? Don't say another word."

"Dad!"

"What?"

"Did you ever wish I was white?"

"Of course not."

"But if you had a white son, wouldn't that make you white too?"

Joseph coughed and said nothing.

"That's logical," Derrick went on. His voice was nasal and thin with mockery. "Wow, Pop, that's a wild fantasy."

"I don't know what you're talking about." The light turned green. "That makes no sense."

"Hurry up!" snarled Derrick. "I want to get to Grandma Grace's house."

Macon Summerscale adjusted his hips beneath the sweaty weight of Sammy's body. Sammy scratched his ear and rolled a bit. A cockroach, missing an antenna, crawled out from between them and disappeared down a cigarette hole in the ancient mattress.

"Stay still awhile," Sammy whispered.

"You funky," said Macon. He kicked up with his heel, brushing Sammy's lanky calf to the side. Someone coughed in the room next door. There was a holler on the hotel staircase, and Macon leapt up, startled on the mattress, causing Sammy's penis to slip greasily out of his ass.

"Damn, man. Why you so jumpy? It's just that ol' nutty drag queen."

"We gotta get out of this rathole," said Macon.

"Takes money for that, bro'."

"Let's rob a store."

"Naw. Git caught." Sammy rubbed his palm on Macon's scalp. "Your hair is still falling out."

115

Macon stood and wiped his ass with the pillowcase. Then he sat back down and gave Sammy a kiss. "Who cares? I got too much hair anyway." He pulled on his blue jeans, caked black on the knees with dirt, and then his only pair of socks, worn translucent in the toes. Sammy rubbed up and down his back with his knuckles.

"What are all these red spots?"

Macon flinched under the touch of cold bent bone. He had dreamt of Provincetown that morning.

"I used to live in a mansion on the water in Provincetown. Sky Daddy's house."

"Sky Daddy?"

"Sugar daddy. 'Cept we got sky instead of sugar."

"H?"

"Cocaine, Special K. H was too messy for Sky Daddy."

"Good old days, huh?"

"Yeah. I used to live on the Upper West Side too," he said. "In a high-rise apartment with my rich black lover, Joe."

"I know Joe. Can't you remember?"

"Man. I'd sit ass-crack naked in a beach chair on the terrace, sipping Johnnie Walker Red. Ol' Joe giving me head."

"You should go to a doctor." Sammy glanced down at the irritated ridge of his own brown penis.

"I'm going back to Joe. I broke his heart when I left."

"I thought he kicked your ass out."

"Yeah. Whatever. I'm still going back."

"**I**t's very free, the gay life," Joseph muttered philosophically, stirring his drink with his pinky. He was trying to get drunk, but he felt more ill than intoxicated. His belly was jumpy. He had skipped dinner, hoping an empty stomach might conspire with the booze to murder his nerves, which had been punishing him with a zealot's relish.

Derrick had refused his telephone call to Brooklyn for the third straight morning. Now his whole life had been called into question — a life he had thought was going fairly well a week ago. He was healthy in his late thirties, an entrepreneur, black and gay, with a Caucasian boyfriend half his age — what did he think he was doing? Breaking every taboo he could think of, it appeared. But he had always been that way. Disdainful of boundaries, obsessed with freedom. Now he felt as sure of his future as a mate on a ship captained by an irreverent drunk.

He turned and grumbled inaudibly to Douglas Seasons, who had accompanied him to the Wonder Bar on East Sixth Street.

"What are you talking about, Joseph?" asked Douglas, signaling to the barkeep for another drink.

"Tell me something, Douglas," Joseph hiccuped. "Should I be allowed the freedom to wreck my life?"

Douglas shook his head. "You're drunk."

But Joseph didn't feel drunk at all, and he was angry at the vodka for not working. "Well, I'm going outside to jump in front of a Yellow Cab," he said.

"Yes, you'll look lovely with tread marks across your face."

"You want to buy the business, Douglas? Because I'm ready for a nervous breakdown."

"I couldn't handle Dolores and Paulie by myself."

"You're forgetting Caleb."

"Him I could handle. Throw him in and I'll think about it."

"You can have him." Joseph had decided that his fatuous, irrational white child lover was the source of all his troubles.

"You know, he is looking. For another man."

"I know. My son upsets him for some reason."

"I wouldn't let him get away. He's a walking wet dream, Joseph. He came in last week in shorts. That kid has the smoothest legs I have ever seen. The curve at his kneecap — Michelangelo would have lost his mind trying to get just that perfect erotic nuance."

Joseph swirled the ice in his drink, glaring at Douglas with a shadowy, dull menace. "We had unsafe sex, you know. The first time we fucked. I couldn't stop myself. Now we just French kiss. Or we use one of these things." He reached into the bowl of complimentary condoms on the bar and held one daintily between two fingers, then dropped it on the floor.

"You're drunk, Joseph."

The bartender came with Douglas's vodka martini. After Douglas paid him, he stood in front of Joseph, drumming his fingers on the bar. "Are you having another drink, sir?" he asked.

"We're both all right," said Douglas. The bartender walked huffily to the far end of the bar.

Disappointment is what I feel, Joseph thought, putting a finger on at least one of his potluck of unpleasant emotions. He was sick with disappointment. His son was gone, and he was afraid they would never speak again. And his infuriating boyfriend was an absolute pain in the ass. Joseph looked around the bar. He was the only person there who wasn't white. Several of the patrons wore black boots, denim mini-cutoffs. Some wore wire-rim glasses. Most of them appeared well-conditioned. Some wore the insignia of ACT UP. "Act up, fight back, fight AIDS," Joseph shouted, pumping his fist into the air. The bartender stared for a moment and then smiled. Two men passing on their way to the back room snickered.

"That did it, Joseph," said Douglas. "I'm driving you home."

"I'm not drunk." Joseph nestled his butt into his barstool. "I'm just...very relaxed."

"Well, whatever. You certainly can't drive in this state." Douglas stood up and pulled on his jacket. "Give me your car keys, Joey."

After Douglas dropped him off at home, Joseph made himself a pot of herbal tea. He flipped through his collection of compact discs — there was the fatal Chili Peppers disc. Then he remembered that Derrick had thrown his CD player over the terrace. He searched his record collection until he found John Coltrane's *A Love Supreme.* "Perfect," he whispered. He put on the album and settled into the black leather love seat in his living room. There was a quiet explosion of cymbals, followed by sweet, mad piano harmonies, then the mystical announcement by the tenor saxophone. He listened to *A Love Supreme* only rarely; he saved it for his hardest or most trying meditations — his brother's death, the first case of AIDS among his friends. He sipped his tea, which was still too hot, threw back his head, and, imagining himself a star navigator, prepared to search within the universe of his soul.

He made one discovery right away. The emotion that had been making him ill all evening was anger. He was furious at Derrick. It wasn't a familiar feeling; he saw his son too rarely to get very mad at him often. There was one time, when Derrick and another boy were accused of trapping a third-grade girl in the back stairway at school and ripping off her panties. Joseph had screamed into the telephone for fifteen minutes, long distance to Cincinnati. Derrick was apologetic, mumbling about a talk with the guidance counselor. That was the year that Racine reclaimed custody, after Derrick had spent three years with his father.

"He's having a hard time," Racine told him on the phone. "He misses you."

Joseph's anger had vanished at that. In its place had come a sinking deadweight of guilt.

He was angry now because, evidently, Derrick doubted his love. The boy was so demanding. He had tried his best, all the boy's life. Still, he had been only a part-time father. What did that mean? Should he have given up his gay life, his chance for happiness with Caleb, and moved to Cincinnati to marry Racine? That was never even think-able. But how could Derrick understand that when he was a child — or now?

Joseph wasn't sure just what was bothering Derrick any-way? Was it sex? Was it race? Was it Caleb's age?

Did you ever want a white son, Dad?

No, he never had, Joseph reassured himself. *No, I never wanted to be white.*

His son's separatism had always worried him. Once on the Great Meadow in Central Park, where Joseph wanted to spread a picnic lunch, Derrick objected at the sight of the sunbathers. "I don't want to be near those white people," he said, his small arms crossed, nine years old at the time. The same summer, when Joseph took him shopping for pants and sweaters, in the department store dressing room Derrick

121

snickered at a white boy his age, eyed him with challenge, and nearly shoved the other boy out of his way.

Joseph argued with Racine over how she was raising his child. "What are you teaching him?" he exclaimed into the telephone. "How can he make it in business if he grows up a black radical?"

"There was a problem at his school. A gang of white kids beat up a black boy. There was real trouble."

"But he can't blame the entire white race."

"He has to know his history, Joseph. I'm seriously considering Islam, myself."

"You're not preparing him for real life," he countered futilely. It was so frustrating, trying to raise a kid by long-distance telephone.

Coltrane was in relentless flight, exploring nether spaces. Hypnotized by the horn, Joseph drifted into a stonelike sleep. He dreamed that he was walking on air and that dogs — short-haired and gray, with yellow-brown teeth — were leaping up and biting at his heels. He could hear their jaw joints working, hard bone snapping shut, spittle gurgling like boiling soup. The dogs hated him, and it was terrible. Joseph lingered purposely in this awful place, to punish himself. The dogs leaped higher, nearly close enough to get him.

He half awoke into a half-dream state, where he could still hear the drums and saxophone, but his mind's eye was dark. He stayed here for a long while, listening to jazz, slipping glacially back into dreams, not of terrors now but of things calm and sweet, images so vivid they lived as words, and memories:

Lying atop the boy, I felt as if I were lying facedown in a running stream of hot water. I could almost taste the hot water splashing into my mouth, rolling over the back of my neck. But there was no water, only the gullible boy beneath me. "Just this once," I whispered. I sucked in my breath so quickly that it burned my tongue.

Did you ever wish I was white, Dad?

Don't you tell him, Joseph. Don't you tell...

I miss my little boy. We had two German shepherds that were mother and daughter. Derrick and I took them for walks, I with the full-grown mother, Nici, and Derrick with the springy, undisciplined puppy he had named Natasha. Tourists stopped to take photos of us. Mother and daughter, father and son. Little and big.

We walked along the waterfront. (Even then I recklessly exposed him to my gay world.) Our walks on the river were perfect. I could feel at a pinpoint in my chest the dawning of a happiness that could reach to the core of the setting sun. I felt proud with my boy at my side, his hand in mine, my arm over his shoulder. People looked at me admiringly, and I drank their admiration.

123

It hurts so much. It's terrible.

No, I don't. No, I never did.

Derrick's voice sang like a robin's. He couldn't speak without singing, and his pitch was precisely tuned to enchant. (A virtuoso might go mad pursuing that tone on a clarinet.) In his clarinet voice he complained that I was mean when I spanked his naughty puppy for chewing my loafers. Later at dinner I found myself debating animal rights from a child's point of view, his seven-year-old's argument as sharp as a solicitor's. I had to concede I had mistreated the dog. I could see his mother (or was it my mother, Grace?) in his face then, his brow knitted fiercely, a force of breath backing his words.

You keep that a secret.

Oh, God, it hurts so much.

Joseph awoke suddenly, jerking up from the love seat's cushions. Coltrane was shrieking and soaring, and the pianist had engineered a bizarre new cosmos of harmony. Joseph lay back and closed his eyes. His mind shimmered within, resonating with the jazz. He inhaled, exhaled, and his breath became electric.

Did you ever wish I was white?

124

No, I don't. No, I never did.

And what about Caleb? Douglas Seasons was in love with his boyfriend, Joseph had realized tonight. Before Douglas left that evening, they sat and talked about his lover. Douglas seemed terribly interested in him and had no shortage of opinions:

"You see, Caleb thinks you're trying to hurt him. It's like you're rubbing his face in his pain — that his real father doesn't love him."

"But Caleb doesn't like his father," said Joseph, listening intently.

"It's not that simple. Derrick strips the mask off of your relationship. He shines a spotlight on how strange it all is — the race thing, the age difference. You don't mind if I'm frank?"

"Not at all, Douglas."

"I mean, there has to be a reason. And a white man your age — it would be so obvious. But a lover of a different race obscures the symbolism. The incest."

Joseph flinched.

"Then along comes your real son and pow! It's in his face again. How his father skewered his guts." Douglas gestured obscenely with a closed fist.

"Oh, Douglas, it hurts so much."

"I know it does, Joseph. When someone you love is in pain."

Joseph frowned. He was talking about Derrick, how rejected he felt by his son, how much *that* hurt, which he thought was the general theme of the evening. But Douglas had assumed he was commiserating with Caleb.

He went into the kitchen to pour himself a glass of water. When he returned, Douglas looked at him impatiently, anxious to continue talking. He sat down on the sofa, and Douglas turned toward him.

"And he's jealous," Douglas went on eagerly, moving forward to the edge of the sofa. "He sees Derrick getting what he never had, his father's attention. He wants to mean more to you than your own son. Because if that's not true, then your love, Joe, is no substitute for his father's. He still comes up short."

Joseph stood up, angry and wobbly, and asked Douglas to leave.

"Psychogibberish," Joseph muttered now as Coltrane flew like a bird up a Dorian scale. "Douglas doesn't know what he's talking about." Joseph resented psychoanalysis, whether the thumbnail or professional variety. He'd walked out on two therapists himself, the last one after an angry shouting match. "Pseudo-Freudian fertilizer."

Joseph didn't know why he was angry at Douglas. He resisted an urge to drink more alcohol. Still he wasn't well, and he needed something. He clasped his fingers to the bridge of his nose, then slapped his hand on the cushion in frustration.

The music stopped playing. Joseph thought he might write a letter to Derrick. He went to his desk and pulled out a sheet of paper and a felt pen. Nothing came to him at first, except "I love you, Derrick. I love you like a thunderstorm. I miss you." Then he wrote Derrick's name over and over down the sheet of paper. He picked up the paper, crumpled it in his hand, opened it again, and stared at it. "He doesn't want to hear this. This would only make things worse."

It was very late. Joseph lit a candle on his desk and pulled out his diary. He opened to a note he had written about Caleb last summer, in the fresh passion of infatuation:

Caleb: A bird's shoulders, a girl's hips, and legs God worked on overtime until She got them just right. Toes like pearls, anklebones cupped in my ears. Chafed heels making a cross behind my neck. Long legs everywhere in bed, tying me up.

It was better just to write to himself. Now was not the time to be so honest with his son. He feared where honesty might lead him. In the candlelight and in the awesome silence left by Coltrane's horn, Joseph felt inspired to write. He would try on paper to mend his splintered life, his aching confusion:

July 1996

I love my boy with power and passion. Is that because he's a young man now, the same age as guys I sleep with? He is three months younger than Caleb. I'm surprised that I've been thinking of them as brothers — black and white brothers. That's nonsense, maybe, but sometimes I find it hard to distinguish my love for my two kids.

There is a difference, though. I'm more threatened by the risks Derrick takes. More under his power. I'm afraid of the bottomless reach of my love for him, the infinity of his need, the foreverness of our bond. If I lost Caleb, I would hurt and ache and fret and cry and pace the floor, but I would get over it. But if I lost Derrick (oh, God, please, never), I would drown in whitewater rapids of grief. Bugs and snakes would have babies in my brain, and I would die and be resurrected as an insane wretch.

I worry about him. I've seen him cry over me, cry simply at my leaving. Have I done some lifelong damage? Have I loved him enough?

I'm also sure I do love Caleb. His attraction is made of surrender and flowing sweetness. And I know now, I feel a brutal impulse, held in check, that he excites; there's a savage undercurrent to my affection for him, so strong that my restraint in not destroying him is itself an act of love. Still, I feel a tender passion for both my boys.

Joseph felt a coldness run up and down his flesh. There was an uncomfortable vitality in his stomach and around his thighs. He sensed a shadow, a thought darting about behind his head, keeping out of sight. He continued to write.

A tender passion. Any love is passionate when desire exists. I desire Caleb's body; I want it for my own. I desire that my son be safe and well; I lust after his well-being. My desire for his happiness is as passionate as my itch for Caleb's flesh. Both of my boys.

Joseph sighed deeply. Exhausted, he put down his pen, blew out the candle on his desk, and went to bed.

WHITE PEOPLE

Derrick's grandmother called to him from the living room. "Boy, come out here! Your father is on the telephone."

"I don't want to talk to him!" he shouted back. *"Faggot,"* he whispered.

In his old bedroom at his grandmother's, Derrick looked out the window over a grassless, empty lot littered with beer cans and bottles. Motionless, he was in an inwardly vibrant mood. He felt confused, like a child, and he blamed his father and Caleb. Whitey and black together. Honkies and colored people? And *gay*? he swore between his teeth.

It wasn't the first time his father had brought white people into his life. Once before, when he was eleven, Joseph had encouraged him to "mix." Caught between doubt and belief, he had taken his father's word. "We're human first. Not all white people are evil."

"But Mommy says... And Malcolm X—" Derrick's mother was dabbling in Islam at the time. After Racine returned from the Ivory Coast, having seen a hundred children Derrick's age die, the house in Cincinnati had changed. There were flags and books, African hats and clothes. The house took on more color. Black night, red blood, green forest. The colors felt opaque and enclosing and wrapped around Derrick like a blanket.

"But Daddy said..."

His mother cut him off. "Your father can be a child sometimes, honey."

And now Derrick believed her. His father lived in a world of clouds. A dream world where white devils and black loved each other. Where men had sex with each other, and that was fine.

He would never speak to him again. He would never let his father fool him or confuse him or hurt him again.

Derrick rubbed his face vigorously with his palms. Through a gap in the maze of black-faced tenement houses, then past the el train tracks, he could see all the way to the ocean. A sliver of lyrical gray-green showed through roof antennas and telephone lines, peeking back at him as if through a keyhole. It was an old, savage view for Derrick.

Coney Island was out that way, just a mile from the Marcus Garvey Houses.

"White people," he muttered.

A small, shaggy black puppy, his tail feathery and upright, had sniffed at Derrick's sand-dusted ankles. A woman called to the dog in Spanish. Derrick smiled. He was fond of the people who fished off the Coney Island pier, and he came here often with his father to feel a part of their seaside culture. Far out on the pier, a brown man climbed to the top of a lamppost and dived bravely into the ocean, disappearing for an uneasy minute. A crowd of boys applauded when the diver's head pushed out of the water. The diver shook his wet, black hair and swam toward the post of the dock. Derrick looked into the distance at a pair of seagulls having an argument, swooping over the currents, squawking as their paths crossed.

The people around him were speaking Spanish. Derrick listened, his eyelids fluttering in the sun as their words rolled percussively out of their mouths, their language, like a tattoo on a drum, subtly evolved to cause a slight alarm.

He looked to the corner of the pier where a small white boy with shining auburn hair knelt on one knee, concentrating on the workings of his long orange-and-black fishing pole. He was sweaty, in dirty low-top sneakers. His bare ankles were smudged with mud. The sun made him squint as a strong ocean wind fondled his hair. He seemed at home on the pier, unconcerned with his surroundings, focused to the point of frustration on a tangle in his fishing line.

His reddened white skin was unique among the gold and deep-brown Spanish majority, and so to Derrick he was exotic. He stared at him directly. The boy cocked his head, aware that he was being watched. Suddenly he looked up and shot a glistening, miraculous smile in Derrick's direction. Surprised and charmed, Derrick turned curious about the fishing pole; he hadn't one of his own. He walked over as the

135

boy wiped his fishing rod with a cloth, his head bent over, inspecting the wheel and handle.

"What kind of pole is that?" asked Derrick.

"It's made out of bamboo."

A sound on the wind touched Derrick's ear. He could barely make out his name being called. He looked toward the shore. His father was on the beach waving at him.

"Who is that?" asked the boy.

"My father."

"You have a fishing rod?"

"Nope."

"You should get him to buy you one."

"I will."

"Here. Sit down and hold mine."

Derrick ducked under the rail and hung his legs over the edge of the pier, careful of splinters. The Spanish diver had climbed to the top of the lamppost again. Sun-slowed, Derrick watched him flex, bend, and prepare to dive. There was a nudge at his shoulder, distracting him just as the diver jumped. It was his new friend offering him the fishing rod.

"How do I hold it?"

The boy positioned Derrick's wrists on the rod, then showed him how to spin the wheel with a finger.

"You out here all alone?" Derrick asked.

"My uncle has a house. See it." The boy pointed shore-ward. "He's retired."

"He's old?"

"No, he's disabled."

136

Derrick studied the boy's face as he told how a loose bolt from a police chopper had fallen from the sky on his uncle's head. He seemed both robust and casual, doll-like in his sweetness as he told the terrible story. Derrick felt sympathy for the mildly odd boy and for his uncle, who had suffered mild brain damage.

"How about your father?"

"My real dad is dead. I just got a stepfather." The boy stood up. "My name is Terry Redwing," he announced.

"I'm Derrick Grant."

"Pleased to meet you."

Terry ran a finger down Derrick's shoulder and arm. "You're sweating."

Derrick thought this was a strange thing to do. He suspected that Terry might have problems with other kids in school. Back in Cincinnati, Derrick's friends would make fun of Terry; sooner or later they would beat him up. And Derrick would have joined in, beating and laughing at the white boy. But out here on the pier, under the vast sky and sun, with his father watching, he felt differently. Terry's manner was fresh and trusting. Derrick decided he liked him.

"We're the only two people out here who aren't Spanish," said Terry.

"I like how Spanish people talk," answered Derrick.

Terry was silent a moment. "I thought that was why you picked me to talk to."

They stayed on the pier until late afternoon, hurling pebbles at gulls, marveling at the Spanish diver, and taking turns fishing. It was the first time in his life Derrick had ever talked to a white boy other than to preen and threaten. Joseph came out onto the pier as the sky turned gold, and the boys said good-bye. Joseph suggested they stay in touch. Derrick bashfully agreed.

So they called each other and met to play in the city. They fought daylong battles in video parlors; they sat making chocolate and strawberry messes in ice cream shops. Walking down city streets, they made fun of every young girl they came across, Derrick lustily and Terry with disinterested sarcasm.

There is something grand about two boys growing close. Hunched over video games, the easy twist of their bodies — a turned ankle, a hip impossibly bent; all moisture, grace, and springy muscle. Terry and Derrick tickled each other's armpits. They bayed like little dogs, frightening grown-ups as they sprinted down the avenue. Their favorite place was the shady cul-de-sac on West 72nd Street, close to the river. They ducked between parked cars, and from there they slipped down a mossy hill into a world of shining, dirty water and tall trees and ran like forest imps along the riverbank.

Weeks into the summer, Joseph asked Derrick about his new friend over breakfast. Derrick could feel a pointed strength in his father's interest, and, ambivalently, he basked in his father's approval of his acquaintance with a white boy.

"I'm going over to his house today," said Derrick.

"Are you? Good."

"Just for lunch. Can you drive me? They live by Central Park."

"You'll meet his parents?"

"So can you."

Joseph washed both their plates in the sink. Suddenly he turned and looked sternly at Derrick. "You behave yourself, hear me? Mind his mother and father, and show respect."

After breakfast and his morning chores, Derrick rode with his father to the gray-front apartment building on Central Park West. The lobby was old and lavish. On a polished wooden table sat a gold vase filled with flat green leaves and tea roses. There was a long carpet with Arabians, like the one his father had, though thicker and softer. The elevator doors were painted gold. The doorman looked funny, Derrick thought, a cross between a clown and a policeman.

"The Redwings, please," Joseph said solemnly to the door-man. Derrick tugged on his father's shirt.

"No, Dad, the Tates. His mother got married again."

"Pardon me, the Tates."

His father's politeness irritated Derrick. "It's just goofy Terry, Dad," he said in the elevator, recalling how his friend had tripped on a pothole and spilled milk shake on Derrick's shirt, making a gang of schoolgirls laugh at both of them.

Upstairs, Terry opened the door. "Hi, Derrick," he cried shrilly. He seemed agitated this morning. "Hi, Mr. Grant?" Derrick felt mysteriously embarrassed. A thin woman in a

139

tight beige skirt and white blouse, in white running shoes, with a light sweat on her brow, came into the hallway.

"Will you wait for me, young man?" she asked. She sounded angry. Derrick felt a numbness in his back. He wanted to leave right away, to grab Terry, leave the boring adults, and run into the street.

"Mom, this is my black friend Derrick. And his dad, Mr. Grant?"

"How do you do, I'm Doris Tate."

"Please, I'm Joseph." Joseph rested his hands on his son's shoulders. "Our boys met at Coney Island."

"Terry told me," she answered with a dead cheeriness. "Can I offer you some coffee? I'm sure these little devils can find something to do."

"Right, Mom, you two talk. Come on, Derrick."

Terry ran down the hallway to his room. Derrick started to run, then stopped and walked down the hall. He glanced over his shoulder at the two grown-ups moving like autobots toward the sofa.

"Derrick, I'll be back to pick you up at 3 o'clock," Joseph called down the hall. Derrick felt that the firmness in his father's voice wasn't necessary.

The boys walked westward in Central Park until they came to a clearing near a softball field. It was a hot, bright day, and once they were no longer under tree shade, Derrick tossed his head backward and showed his face to the sun. Terry nudged him with his elbow.

140

"Aren't you dark enough already?" He glanced up and down his own pinkish, red-streaked arm. "I'll never catch up with you."

Derrick laughed both inside and out. "Bunk you," he chimed as they climbed into the bleachers to watch two teams of women playing softball.

"Girls run funny," said Terry after a short while.

"They run nice."

"Their hips move sideways."

"That's because of their bones. So they can have babies."

A batter hit a line drive into center field. Derrick sat up excitedly, clapping his hands as the field came alive with hurtling, base-circling womanhood. Terry grabbed onto his arm, hugging him. "There goes Derrick down the first-base line. Holy cow, he's safe!"

Derrick shoved him away. "Leave me alone, you lunar fungus."

"So, you're a moon rock."

"You come from Delta Quadrant."

"You—"

Derrick pinched Terry's earlobe to make him shut up.

"Let's go over there." Terry pointed to the west, a brick underpass partially hidden by a rock hill and a black cinder road that passed through dark shade.

"No. Let's watch the game," said Derrick, eyeing the first basewoman's green culottes.

"I'm sick of looking at girls."

"I like 'em."

"Come on, Derrick!" insisted Terry.

"All right!"

They stumbled over tree roots, over the rock hill onto the cinder bridle path and followed it to the arched underpass. Derrick was bored and wanted to go back to the softball game. Terry dug a chunk of red glass out of the dirt and stared through it at the sun.

"This is boring and dirty," said Derrick.

"Come look at this."

"No."

Out of sight, past the underpass, there was a sound like a firecracker. Then two more muffled explosions and a scream.

"Come over here," said Derrick. But Terry was lost in concentration, hunting for something on the ground. Derrick heard more loud voices. Someone was yelling angrily. *"Don't touch him! Don't touch him!"* He grew alarmed and moved off the bridle path and out of the shade onto the sunlit grass.

"Come here, Terry."

Terry was down on his knees. He'd found another piece of colored glass imbedded in the dirt. Derrick looked south toward the loud noise. Past the rock hill now, in the sunlight, a police officer was running on the grass. Derrick took a deep, fearful breath. Now he could hear it: galloping hooves, the high-pitched fire breath. "Terry!" he shouted.

From beneath the underpass the horse appeared as a storm of cinder dust and a snorting, meaty mass hurtling toward the minuscule boy. Terry made one quick pivot on his knee. The animal was a second away, and Terry still might have escaped, but he rolled backward and fell on the ground. On his back, eyes skyward, Terry gasped, "No." Quietly, not a scream; rather in a speaking voice but loud enough for Derrick to hear. Then he rose up on his elbows just before an iron-clad hoof struck him squarely in the head.

The horse seemed stymied by the tiny obstacle under its hooves. Stumbling to a stop, it stepped on a limp hand, then kicked at the boy's head with its hind legs. The beast wandered toward the brick wall along the edge of the park. It pranced halfheartedly in a circle, bumping stupidly into the wall. Terry was facedown on his belly, his head and arms motionless, both of his legs shivering.

The policeman came running through the underpass. He stopped near Terry for a moment, then stood and walked slowly toward the horse, his hands shaking, with his firearm drawn. The animal reared once, its eyes flaring insane and bright. The officer fired into its chest, and it gave an abrupt snort and dropped to the ground. The policeman fired again and then turned and ran back to Terry's fallen body.

At the sound of the gunfire, at the sight of the glass-eyed, dying beast, Derrick panicked. His cheeks convulsing, half blind with shock, he took a step toward his friend on the ground.

"Get back, you black—!" screamed the cop, waving his arm hysterically. "Get the hell back!" The officer's nose, as dark as a plum, appeared about to burst. Stunned by the deep, red color, Derrick stepped back on the grass.

143

A quiet minute passed while the officer spoke incoherently into his radio. A crowd of watchers came near, surrounding Derrick suddenly, shoving him forward to the edge of the bridle path. Soon sirens were sounding in the near distance.

"What happened?" an onlooker asked.

"Some guy took a shot at the mountie," a voice offered. "The horse threw the cop and went crazy."

Police cars and an ambulance van pulled up onto the grass. Two paramedics ran to Terry's body. They worked rapidly, padding blood with towels, yanking instruments out of their bags. Two other men in white stood nearby with a stretcher.

"Turn him over!"

"You can't move him yet."

"There's a pulse. You have to turn his head."

"You can't move him yet!"

They hovered over the child, their backs to the crowd, hiding Terry from view. Their movements, from behind, appeared quick and tense. Then one of the paramedics stood up from the ground and flung his head to the side in a gesture of failure and grief. At the mortal gesture Derrick caught spit in his nostrils and choked. He knelt down in the grass in the middle of the crowd.

"Are you all right?" an old woman asked.

He looked up into her face, a hacking cough pushing from his chest. Behind the crowd Derrick heard a woman screaming. He stood up shakily and turned to see Mrs. Tate running on the bridle path. Derrick remembered the woman softball players.

For a brief moment he felt as if he were drowning in boiling water. He lost control of his spasming eyelids. Then he dropped to his knees on the grass and fainted.

He woke up to an ammonia scent, his head in the puffy hands of a paramedic. The ambulance was gone. Terry's body was gone also. The crowd had thinned to just a few hangers-on. A small circle of policemen stood collegially over the horse, one lightly kicking the dead animal's snout with his shoe. A police officer drove Derrick home in a blue-and-white.

Derrick had been to only one funeral before, his maternal grandmother's down in Virginia. He was eager to see Terry's body laid out, just as his grandmother's had been, in a shapely coffin with beautiful borders carved into the wood and around it a rainbow of plant life. At the funeral in Virginia, all day his mother ordered him to sit still and keep quiet. He had felt like a pest. Now he would be a guest of honor, consoled especially by the reverend, handshakes from everyone, for he was the bereaved. He *was* the beloved, the deceased's best friend. Terry's uncle knew that. His mother knew it too. Why hadn't anyone called with the time and place? It had been seven days.

"Wouldn't the body start to rot by now?" he asked his father.

Joseph fumbled for an excuse. He had spoken to Terry's stepfather. "It might be just for the family."

"No teachers? No school friends? That doesn't make any sense, Dad."

"Things get confused at a time like this. They're in shock. His mother probably hasn't stopped crying yet."

But Terry had told Derrick the truth just two weeks before in Riverside Park. "My stepfather doesn't like black people. He calls them names." His arms slung over the branch of a small tree, Terry had stared at him with an ashlike expression in his eyes. "I'm not like him."

Derrick looked up at his father, his feet squared, his small arms crossed. Then he relaxed his posture. "At least we sent them flowers."

"Yes. And Terry knows, Derrick."

The next morning Derrick told his father he was going down to the river to watch the ducks. He was lying; he really planned to go pay his respects to Terry's mother. And to tell her he understood; it was okay that the funeral was for family only. Perhaps he could visit the grave with his father. Could she tell him, please, where he was buried?

Derrick walked along the river until it dipped under a bridge beneath the highway. The bank dwindled to an impassable spread of pebbles. He scrambled up a soft dirt hill, stepped out onto the cul-de-sac on 72nd Street, and walked the several crowded city blocks until he reached Central Park West. From there it was a short walk to the Tates' apartment house. He didn't remember the address. Door by door he looked for the gold vase of tea roses and the doorman with the red mustache.

146

Finally he came to a familiar glass front, looked up, and, yes, he did recognize the short man with the gray policeman's cap. Derrick tapped on the glass. The doorman looked at him with a blank expression. He waved his hand and mouthed the words, "Get away."

"May I see the Tates?" Derrick mouthed back. The doorman's blankness turned strange. He opened the door.

"Go away, little boy. You have the wrong house."

"No, I don't. I'm looking for Mrs. Tate."

"What do you want with Mrs. Tate?"

"To pay my respects."

"Oh, for the little boy. My God, it was horrible."

Derrick winced. In his mind he saw Terry's calf kicking in the dirt, his eyes glistening. And the body of the horse surrounded by police when he woke up from fainting.

"How do you know the Tates?" asked the clown-cop.

"The little boy was my friend."

"From school?"

"Yes," Derrick lied.

"Wait a minute." The doorman spoke a moment on the PA phone, then hung up.

"You wait here a minute," he repeated. Derrick tucked his hands in his pockets and waited.

Inside the building lobby, the elevator door opened. A man in a gray suit stepped out. He had gray hair, blue eyes, a gray mustache. He milled about in the lobby a moment, then came briskly toward the front door.

"Here is Mr. Tate," said the doorman.

"Trouble?"

"Mr. Tate, I'm very sorry. This young fellow says he went to school with your late son."

Terry's stepfather stared at the doorman; then his translucent pupils rotated slowly, like a turret, downward to fix on Derrick.

"I don't know what this is about, but you did not go to school with my son. Now you better get out of here."

"I met Terry on Coney Island. I was with him—"

"This is some nigger scam," he said to the clown-cop. "Can't you handle a little boy?" He looked down again at Derrick, blinked twice, then flashed a small smile. "He's probably a pickpocket. Now get him out of here," he said. He brushed past Derrick, stopped and patted his jacket pocket, and then walked out the front door.

"Get out of here, you black little bastard," said the doorman. "Go away, or I will call the police."

Derrick ran out of the doorway.

"If I see you again, no talk. I just call the police," the clown-cop shouted after him.

That same morning, while Derrick made his way back home in tears along the river, Joseph sat at his desk and wrote and wrote, with all the compassion he thought appropriate, a letter to the dead boy's parents, damning their treatment of his child. It took him the better part of the day. Out of sympathy for their loss, he decided not to post the letter until several months had passed.

Since the death of his friend Terry, Derrick had developed just the slightest loss of spring in his newly teenage step. He still visited his father in the summer, as his mother insisted, but he did not insist himself on spending Christmas or spring vacation from school in New York City.

He was confused: His father had promised after the accident that he could come live with him again. Now a molasses-slow sadness descended over Derrick with every autumn, every trip back home on a plane to Cincinnati — each trip he wasn't supposed to make, by his father's promise. It felt like exile and not the natural cycle of seasons he had known most of his life — New York and his dad at the end of spring, Cincinnati and his mother in the fall. He knew there was a reason his father so eagerly said good-bye to him on airport runways every September, waving hastily, ants in his pants to get back to — what? An image beckoned like a dying constellation in Derrick's memory, a gray dawn in Brooklyn, boys with no pants, men holding hands on the waterfront.

Derrick's legs grew strong between the ages of eleven and fourteen, and though his step lost just a bit of spring, he could still jump higher than any other boy at school. His arms grew strong too. He could do more push-ups and beat everyone at wrestling. His grip grew strong, and his lungs turned into oxygen ovens, powering up with energy that he hoarded like stored explosives. Sometimes he made himself dizzy breathing, only because he loved the feel of his lungs and the burning around his eyes when he pumped them hard and long.

His friends at school — Joe Jr., Dutch, Kenneth, and Peanut — were afraid of Derrick because he was the strongest, and their fear made him smile, though he was certain he would never hurt any of them. But he was also certain that he could if he wanted, and they had better not forget that.

Terry! If anyone could have seen the open wound, the long, uneven gash crusted with powdered blood, sheared skin tinted with rust, the emotional scar with small pools of pus still dripping.

"Try not to think of it," repeated the therapist over and over. That was all she could say. It was all he remembered her ever saying.

Racine pored over the long list of medicines, finally deciding which was the best for her daughter's bronchitis. Behind her against the wall in the shadows, Derrick looked at his half sister, Steffa, with eager affection, his shoulders tensed, anticipating her next outburst. The four-year-old's crying excited him. His bones shivered with each scream out of the child's lungs.

"There, there, baby. Sugar, sugar." His mother seemed to smother the girl, her arms wrapped around the tiny head until the face disappeared. Derrick peeked over her shoulder at the round reddish-brown face, the pink lips, the eyelids white with tears. Then he clasped his hand on his mother's shoulder and turned to leave.

"Be back, Ma."

"Derrick, come back here, boy." But he had vanished, as he often did lately since returning home from New York.

Outside Derrick ran hard to the handball courts ten blocks away. Three white boys walked past him. He peered into their faces. The summer had brought such change — he wasn't sure if he recognized the one in the middle with the pale streak in his hair. The boy he fought with the spring before.

I thought he was trying to steal my sister.

Last spring Derrick had taken Steffa for a walk. Joe Jr. and Peanut had come down the street with a new stickball bat. "Let Derrick try it," cried Peanut, who was afraid of Derrick and wanted to appease him. Peanut's mother had two husbands, and the one she had chased out into the street with a hot curling iron still brought him gifts, like this red stickball bat with gold stripes on the handle.

"Fresh!" said Derrick. He gripped the gold stripes and waved the bat, feeling it cut the air. "Today is your doom,

Obi-Wan," he said, deepening his voice until it hurt. Then he balanced the stick on his fingertips and turned around to show his little sister how cool he was. But she was gone!

Derrick took off, running as fast as he could to the corner. He looked one way and then the other. Glimpsed through an alley all the way to the railroad tracks. No sign, and she couldn't have gotten that far. So he turned right and ran to the next corner. To the left, nothing. To the right Steffa was walking toward him, and a white teenage boy was holding her hand.

"Steffa!" Blindly Derrick charged the boy, yanked his hand away from his little sister's and pushed his forearms into the boy's face. They both hit the ground hard.

"I was bringing her back," the boy cried between choked breaths. Derrick thought of Steffa. He was making the same mistake, not watching her. He jumped up from the ground and took her in his arms.

By now Joe Jr. and Peanut had arrived with the stickball bat. Joe Jr. waved the stick menacingly. Peanut danced about, waving half-open fists. The white boy crawled up to his knees, held his head, and then stood up.

"I was bringing her back. I knew she was lost. She pointed the way."

Derrick held his sister close to him. He ran his hand through her hair and touched her bows. Then he turned to his friends. "Let's get out of here."

"You better watch yourself," Joe Jr. shouted at the white boy, pointing a finger.

"Yeah, get outta here," cried little Peanut, shaking a limp fist.

"I thought he was stealing my sister," Derrick told Joe Jr. as they walked away. "I made a mistake."

"I was gonna fuck him up," said Peanut.

"Peanut, you warn't going to do shit," said Derrick.

The pale streak in brown hair was new, but there was a wince of recognition in the boy's face. Derrick felt a numbing regret at having blamed that boy for Terry Redwing's parents. Or was it Terry he blamed — for making friends with him in the first place, for not being hateful like other whites and at least keeping things clear and simple? As Derrick walked past, he stared at the one boy with an invented look on his face, his mouth turned downward, his eyes firm yet soft. For a moment, he felt a terrible fatigue.

He spent the afternoon at Joe Jr.'s house playing handball and reading the stack of *Playboys* Joe Jr.'s father kept hidden under the kitchen sink.

It was near dark when he got home. He heard voices in the kitchen. It was his mother's friend Sondra, her tonk partner on Friday nights.

"So if you knew, why did you sleep with him?"

"I wanted him."

"You thought you could change him?"

"I never thought of that. I *wanted* him. He used to stand naked in front of his window doing tai chi, and from my room I could see him."

"With binoculars?"

153

"I'm going to slap you in a minute. But, no, he was fine. He ran track instead of lifting weights like the other brothers, and his body was *sweet*. I'd see him coming from the woods all by himself. This was an unusual brother. It turned me on. And always talking about freedom. That's how I knew. Why else would his freedom mean so much to him? And *that* turned me on. That he wanted men to do that to him. And didn't even know it himself. Not yet."

"But why did you get pregnant?"

"I'm not the first woman to get knocked up without knowing it."

"*I* think you planned it in the subconscious. A baby but no ball and chain. No man lying 'round the house farting and scratching his johnson. And child support too? Beats the sperm bank, honey." Sondra slapped the table twice. "Hah, hah!"

"I thought of that. Tell you the truth, I was just after some good nooky."

"*I* think you are a lesbian. I read about this in *Essence*. Women that like sweet men, deep down you are really lesbians."

"You can go home now, Sondra."

Derrick ran quietly upstairs to his room, wondering if his mother had been talking about Steffa's father or his own.

After Sondra left, Racine turned on the radio and rolled herself a fine marijuana cigarette. Her children, Derrick and Steffa, were asleep.

The radio was in the middle of a long jazz sojourn by her favorite sax player. He was among a handful of the greatest musicians in the world, both by repute and in Racine's opinion. Though he wasn't always musical. Much of what he did with his horn, he did because it felt good to play it, not for a beautiful sound. No other jazzman imposed his physicality — his tongue, his breath — into his listener's ear this way. Racine could feel him sucking and fluttering his reed. It occurred to her that he was likely a virtuoso at oral sex as well, and for a silly moment she imagined him playing her vagina like a horn. She stepped out onto her porch so the children wouldn't smell the grass and left the door cracked to hear the music.

Steffa was better. She considered the money she saved by being able to treat her child herself. But Derrick, her fourteen-year-old...boy. Boy, boy. Her baby man, still traumatized by the violent death he had witnessed and what happened after. Her own distrust, her anger at Joseph (she was *right all along*) had made it difficult for her to help her son grieve for his dead white friend. The therapy sessions had ended a year ago. Now it was her job to fix Joseph's mess.

Still, she had no great regrets about Joseph. She couldn't imagine Derrick with another man's DNA, and she wouldn't change anything about the boy she adored more than she had ever loved a man.

She was a scientist; that colored everything she did. In a way Derrick's blood was her experiment. What if the father were gay? This was her unconscious hypothesis. What if the father's heart had never been broken by a woman? No woman had ever sexually rejected Joseph. He may have been jealous of girls who got the boys he wanted. But that would make him madder at boys than girls. So Derrick would get a fresh start. He wouldn't inherit misogyny from his father. Though to some extent she knew he would learn it on his own.

So much he would have to discover on his own. He would have to invent his own manhood, as she had invented her womanhood. And she could see it already — Derrick *creating* his sexuality, not learning from his queer father to fuck women, to begrudge women, to fear women. It thrilled her. She applauded her own daring and her vision. She had started a revolution.

The one thing she trusted in Joe Grant was that he would fight over only what he truly believed. He never fought just to fight, as her father had. Her mother fought back, and the marriage didn't last long enough to mean anything to Racine. She barely remembered it.

"Ma?"

Derrick was coming down the steps. She stepped on the marijuana cigarette and fanned her breath.

"Out here, Derrick."

The saxophone colossus was honking about his time on the islands. It reminded her of her years in the Ivory Coast. Racine smiled at how handsome her boy was in his bathrobe and bare feet. She saw him one day as a husband, the father of many children. Her face flushed a bit.

156

The sax player puffed out a candle and was silent. Derrick joined her on the porch. She put her arm around his head and kissed it and held him close in the night.

She had stood likewise with her arm around the shoulders of Nana, the chief's son, her last day in the Ivory Coast. Of course, the strong African made her think of her son, of the young man she wanted him to become. She had held Nana warmly, with affection and hope, but then coldly to keep back both of their passions.

Her sex with the twenty-year-old had ended weeks before, once she had decided not to stay in Africa but to return home to America. Nana had momentarily convinced her to stay. He had convinced her with his love and lovemaking and his complex of needs as intricate as a tree's improvisation of life. At first Racine could see no end to it — there was no clear aim in loving Nana. The day they met she knew it would hurt when she had to leave him. Briefly she considered a revolution in her life — a wedding. Then she changed her mind. Even as she stood with her arm around him, looking over the horizon of *l'Côte Ivoire* from the terrace of Nana's bedroom, he tried one last time to persuade her to stay.

But it was too risky, she knew.

He was born to power — as the chief's son he would sit on the cabinet. "I will be the minister of state — no, the minister of science."

She laughed. She could not imagine this ever being, Nana was such a boy still, though she knew he spoke the truth. But he had so much to sort out yet.

"I hate capitalism," he would say on Tuesday, dressed in neo-Marxist camouflage and black beret. On Thursday, drunk with wine and erect with the power of his future, Nana changed his song. "When I am the minister, I will be driving a Mercedes," and the buzz of his African brogue and his powerful young erection made her pores open in lustful sympathy.

She loved about him the rich, boundless black of his skin — so rare in America, such purity. She felt assaulted by his great promontory cheekbones. In bed she loved the way he gobbled her clitoris like a starving man ("Bad table manners," she laughed), the foreign dialect that he spoke to her labia.

In lovemaking Nana had studied the hunting technique of the heron. He had stolen its stealth, the gentle footfall into mud so as not to disturb the water where his unalerted prey swam about. Then the stab, always by surprise. She never knew when he would strike. And so she felt hunted each time in bed. Only once did she outguess him and anticipate his single thrust. She didn't climax that time and looked at him sadly disappointed that she had won their game. But only once. Nana never betrayed himself again. The slow press, a

159

slow peeling, the flapping heron's wings, in and out, in and out, then the sudden, wonderful strike. Nana was so satisfying, so beautiful.

And charismatic and wealthy and fortunate. Racine was excited but also frightened by the confusion that was his birthright as a member of African aristocracy. The chief of the N'bum tribe was his father. In America that would be a governor or the mayor of a large city. His family fortune, in timberland, was greatest during the worst times for his country. His great-grandfather had collaborated with the French colonialists, signing deals and stealing land. Racine knew better than to mention this ever. It was the controversy, the danger and doubt in his bloodline: his great-grandfather on his mother's side.

Because he was his mother's son, Nana had enemies whose hatred dated back long before his birth. Men who wanted to end that bloodline forever. Yet he seemed more vexed by his mother's control over his destiny than by the men who thought they could redeem their nation's soul by hanging him.

"I don't want her love," he raved once he trusted Racine. "She loves weakness. If she loves you, it means you are weak."

Under a cotton sheet, naked against her lover, her feet tangled in his thighs, Racine made a silent promise to her eight-year-old son on the other side of the world that when he grew up she would love his strength. She would never ransom his manhood with love.

"I won't be happy until Mikaka doesn't love me. To be worthy of her love is to be nothing," repeated Nana.

Racine loved Nana, but his passionate conflicts with his family made her pause in letting her feelings run free.

All day she studied blood. She drew it from babies, from large round wombs, nervous fingertips, fat folded buttocks, cramped muscles. From drowsing ancients and crying newborns and from those alert enough to search her face for their fate, as if she could tell from the color of their blood, the force with which it leapt into the needle, its smell, or just from the way their hands shook with worry.

But she couldn't tell. And if she could, she would have dismissed it. She knew nothing until she had passed their blood through filters, mixed it with chemicals, boiled and froze it, and watched the microscopic shapes dancing like wild animals under a lens and powerful electric light. Then looked at the numbers and considered the difference in climate and diet and regional norms. Then ran the tests again and looked under the microscopes again to make certain. And reviewed the numbers.

A bug was being passed through the milk of the local women to their babies. The swelling in the mother's stomach was unnoticeable, though it showed up discreetly in the numbers. In the children's stomachs, though, the swelling was severely painful and caused choking. Her fellowship was to design a protocol advising women for or against nursing. Susceptibility in the babies, the presence of

161

the germ in the mother's body, then in her milk, were her key variables.

She considered each factor like a chess piece; she advanced it to its optimal position relative to the other on a two-dimensional graph, then predicted all possible interactions. Then added in the error margins for each. Racine was one of six funded chemists working in parallel on the same study. An international board of physicians would choose the best protocol and pay to institute that protocol. *More money.*

And that was it — she would win the follow-up grant money, marry Nana, and live forever in Mother Africa as the wife of a cabinet minister. She would renounce her American citizenship and convert to Islam. When her studies were complete, she would bring Derrick to live with her, take him from his queer father who wanted to turn her baby into an artist; Racine would raise him instead as an Islamic prince. It seemed the perfect life plan.

Except Nana was too angry. His campaign against his mother seemed perverse to her. As Elizabeth feared the murder of any anointed queen, even the hated queen of Scots, Racine feared such anger by any son against the woman whose loins he had fractured in birth.

As a scientist she presumed bias on Nana's part, and so she went to visit Mikaka to see what kind of woman she was. Could she become this woman one day? If she became the wife of the future chief, would Derrick grow up like Nana, the chief's son, and despise her love and put his manhood

162

above her? Racine could answer her questions only through observation.

Though Mikaka had not separated formally from Nana's father, she had her own house in Samti province. She was having a breakfast of cucumbers, white wine, and ice when her manservant escorted Racine into the rear garden. The woman was tall, very dark, and voluptuous, with Nana's cheekbones — high vantage points of beauty. Her hair was not yet dressed and hung freely around her neck. She wore only a morning gown with a seam running from left shoulder to right heel; the top was ivory white, the bottom black-and-gold checked. Racine had met her only briefly at the university dinner where she had also met Nana, a year before.

"Do you feel comfortable in our language?" Mikaka asked.

Racine knew only enough to interview patients and to make her away around the rural villages. *"I can't discuss the things I want in your language,"* she struggled.

Mikaka smiled with great interest and delight. She answered, *"With a few words you've told me all you have to."* Then she changed her tongue. "Fine, let's speak English. Have you had breakfast?"

Racine felt slyly challenged by Mikaka's offer. If she ate, she would fumble and appear nervous. If she refused, she would appear cold and uncomfortable, and she did not want to challenge Mikaka. "A pot of tea and perhaps a cup of ice." But "perhaps" came out unnaturally. She resolved not to make any other pretense, for it would put her at a disadvantage.

"Hot tea over ice is wonderful." Mikaka glanced at her servant. He spoke briefly in French and disappeared.

"Nana disappoints me," Mikaka began, without waiting for Racine to talk. "If he doesn't improve, he should not succeed his father. He will be destroyed in the ministry."

Racine was startled, as if the woman had read her mind. She had revealed too much of her mission, as Mikaka said, with just a few words.

"Nana is still young," Racine offered unsurely.

"You're a lovely girl, Racine. You are young also. You think youth is an excuse because you are an American. There are no excuses in *l'Côte Ivoire.*"

"I'm also afraid he is going to be hurt."

"Then take him back to America with you. He should get a doctorate. When he returns I'll make him my flunky in the Department of Agriculture. I could use both of you."

Racine felt overwhelmed by Mikaka's fencing quickness and her sensuality and the dazzling white and checkered gown. The woman was twice her age and seemed vastly experienced. Mikaka's perception was a sickle that would cut her up like dry cabbage if she tried to fool her. The only practical thing, it seemed, was to speak with complete frankness.

"Nana says you want him to be your flunky, like you said. He says you love him only when he is weak, and you always take back your love when he tries to be strong."

"*Flunky* is a beautiful English word. It excites me sexually. You have many sexy sounds in your language."

Now Racine felt insulted. And angry, for she had shown no disrespect or dishonesty to Mikaka.

"Is Nana right?" Racine insisted.

"The boy will die in prison. They will hang him after his father dies. Nana refuses to do anything I want, and that is exactly how I control him. I will whip him until he learns to be a man."

Racine felt exhilarated by Mikaka's bluntness. She felt invited to join her in jettisoning all pretense.

"You are a horrible woman," she exclaimed with great pleasure.

Mikaka smiled with a vast delight. For a moment she gazed over her left shoulder at the green hills and the village in the distance. She poured herself more wine over ice, then leaned forward and without invitation poured wine into Racine's teacup.

"Tell me why I am horrible."

"Because you corrupt love. You use love. And you don't care about your son."

"But my love is my power. It is a bottomless hole Nana is afraid to fall into, afraid he will drop forever. He fights against me, but he is only swinging at mist. Nana is a fool because he fights against his own feelings. And if he cannot beat even me, then he will die in prison. I am a lovely woman. You think I'm horrible because you come from Disneyland."

Racine looked into Mikaka's eyes. They looked to her like platelets, pushing and shoving about under a microscope.

"Why do you love weakness?"

165

"I love Nana's father. His father is not weak."

"Nana can be strong. Why can't you love his strength?"

"Because he hasn't enough of it. If he tries to be strong, my father's enemies will murder him." Mikaka brushed her neck in a gesture of irritation. Her eyes shaded over in calculation. "You have a kid, don't you?"

Racine was silent.

"You think you should be perfect, the perfect mother. More Disneyland."

"I wanted to talk because I need to know about Nana. I couldn't marry him until I know what will happen to him."

"That's a good idea. An American wife, of course. Take him back with you. Make him get his doctorate so I can use him."

"I don't hear any love in that statement."

"I love my son. But I won't make-believe. Nana wants me to make-believe."

"Have you given up on him?"

"Almost," smiled Mikaka. "Not completely."

She leaned forward and poured more wine into Racine's teacup.

"How old is yours?"

"Eight years old."

"A boy? Of course, a boy. And you abandoned him to fly around the world and seduce my son."

"Yes. Ain't I terrible?" Not being a drinker, Racine felt giddy after even one cup of wine.

"You hussy." Mikaka laughed. And Racine laughed from the wine and from the excitement that Mikaka stirred in her.

166

"Don't pretend to love your son any more than you really do, Racine. That does no one any good."

Racine felt naked with Mikaka now. She stopped pretending to herself to feel hostile toward her. For the rest of the morning they drank and laughed about not much of anything. They talked frankly about sex, politics, medicine, and their children. Racine felt wonderful in her company.

Mikaka showed Racine out to the front steps of her house. Her servant looked in surprise that his mistress would show anyone such courtesy other than a state guest. She pointed out to Racine her paintings, encased jewelry, and other artwork as they made their way through rooms and halls.

"Do you appreciate good art?"

Racine said certainly, but truthfully art had never had much meaning to her. She had always thought Joseph's interest in it was unimportant. The modern Americans she knew about only well enough to conduct herself at socials. Of African art she knew nothing.

"I love this piece most of all." Mikaka pointed to an androgynous figure carved in startling black adamant. It was as tall as a man, but the head and belly were the size of an infant's. The face was the shape of a teardrop set on edge — the mouth coming to a menacing point. "And I stole it. The stupid trader didn't know its value. The stone is so hard, it must have taken ten years to carve. I could sell it in America and buy a house for you and Nana.

167

"It gives me energy and power. Touch it." Mikaka rubbed her fingers around its neck. "It's why I buy it. Hands off in a museum, right? Touch it, Racine."

Racine moved her hand toward the mouth, fearful she would cut herself, and tapped her fingertip on the sharp point.

The ride back to her apartment in Abidjan was a leisurely one. Racine asked Nana's driver, Jame, to show her the countryside. He turned off the highway and took a dirt road into the hills.

"What did you think of Mikaka?" Jame asked in halting French.

"I liked her. I was impressed."

"She is dangerous."

"Yes. Do you think she is dangerous for Nana?"

"That's what I meant."

A brief rain poured, lasting a few minutes. Racine rolled down the car window and put her palms out to catch a few drops of water.

"How long have you worked for their family?"

"All my life. My father as well. You come from the United States?"

"Yes."

"Yes? I want to know everything. Tell me your life story in five minutes. Then I will tell you mine."

Racine hesitated, massaging droplets of rain into her palms.

"Come on. Just the important things. You are not that old — it shouldn't be difficult. Or make one up. Make up an American life."

168

"My father…my mother—"

"Five minutes now. Think before you start."

"My father and my mother disagreed about everything. About whether to move north to New York or stay in Virginia. About whether to have an abortion when she became pregnant the fourth time in four years. That would have been my baby brother or sister, but when my mother refused, my father kept at her and then moved out of the house. So she had the abortion while he was away, but then she couldn't forgive him, and they divorced.

"So I grew up seeing my father only a few weeks a year in the summer, in New York. My mother always said bad things about him, but I never believed her. I went to school in Virginia. I fell in love with a boy when I was fifteen. He was my first lover. His name was Benny."

"Two minutes."

"Benny was my boyfriend for three years, but then he got another girl, Rebecca, pregnant, and he had to marry her because her father was a policeman."

"So you cried and cried."

"I guess so. I don't remember."

"Three minutes."

"Virginia is the most beautiful place I have ever seen. Your country is beautiful, but the American South has so much soul. You can feel a hundred years of time in a blade of Virginia grass. Some days I look at the hills and just start to cry. I went to school up north and got pregnant. I never married the man. I have a son. I have a good job. I have hope for the future."

169

"Time up."

"Well, now it's your turn."

"My father was Mikaka's bodyguard. He was murdered in our house as part of a plot to kill her by the families bankrupted by the French and Nana's grandfather. I was two years old. I survived because my mother had carried me with her to Mikaka's house to baby-sit for Nana, just born. Mikaka knew about the plot but never warned my family. Instead she had lookouts at our house. The murderers were caught on the road to her house in Samti and beheaded on the spot. Mikaka gave my mother a house. She gave me a job. I will work for her until she is divorced, deposed, or decapitated."

Later that evening Racine wrote in her diary:

On the front porch of Mikaka's house there was a sculpture. It had a long neck, diamond head, round belly. I stared at it while I waited for Nana's driver. The long neck alarmed me. I felt I was being stretched into the shape of the sculpture.

Behind it in the garden was another sculpture of woman and child, and though it was simply shaped from ovals, in the sunlight it cast a shadow on the white fence exactly like the shadow a real woman would cast. How did the artist predict this? The geometry seems impossible.

I won't marry Nana. Mikaka is right, he will have to become a monster or else be murdered in the cabinet or be her flunky. I'll finish my work and leave. As soon as I can, I want to see Derrick. If I could leave tonight, I would.

I thought hard about marrying him and bringing you there to live, honey. I almost did marry him."

"Africa, huh?" said Derrick.

"You are a prince anyhow. My young prince." Racine kissed Derrick on the cheek and straightened the collar of his bathrobe.

KID
BROTHER

Caleb has lived in the same house in Brooklyn for as long as he remembers. When he was a child, he had his own room — his sanctuary — which he loved. When his parents moved into separate bedrooms (his and his little brother's), they put the two boys together in the master bedroom. Ted and Caleb roomed together for a year. Night after night, Caleb confessed his secrets to Ted. He kept his eyes to himself whenever Ted changed his underwear. When Caleb's mother finally divorced his dad, the boys moved back into their separate rooms. But during the year, Caleb had fallen in love with his baby brother, and changing bedrooms again was traumatic. He has never felt quite the same about his private sanctuary, or about his house, or his neighborhood.

In his room now are his CD collection and portable player, a rack of T-shirts from his all-time favorite rock concerts, a cordless telephone, a New York Yankee yearbook from 1992 signed by their All-Star clean-up batter. A picture of his mother, a yarmulke he hasn't worn since he was twelve, a souvenir Speedo he swiped from the Boy's Club locker room while his favorite day-camp counselor was in the shower. There is a snapshot of him and Joseph hidden under a place mat on the top of his bureau.

Caleb is not there. His father is downstairs, his brother is in the backyard with his girlfriend playing punchball, and whenever his family is home, Caleb tends to stay away:

I can sleep at Joe's house anytime, so I don't need to go home too much. When I do go home, I feel like a ghost stuck inside a wall. I can't talk, just little hints about my actual life. I tell a lot of lies. Now my kid brother Ted, he's lucky. He gets to talk about his girlfriend, this big-mouth bossy brunet babe named Julie. She's decent.

The first time Ted got ever laid, it was so obvious when he walked in the door that Saturday night. He shuffled around the kitchen talking about bull crap, trying to convince me he wasn't hiding anything. I pretended not to suspect. So we talked about baseball and the movies and Poppy's rotten health.

Suddenly Ted asked me to take a walk. Honestly, I had been staying away from him, but his eyes looked so sparkly, I felt sorry for him. Back then I had never felt what he was going through — sexual satisfaction. But now I know. His body was his best friend that night.

Ted wanted to go to Coney Island. It was the biggest night of his life, and he didn't want it to end just yet. It was midnight, but I said okay. I figured he'd tell me about balling his first chick, which I wanted to hear about but sort of didn't.

Where we live in Brooklyn is five blocks from the subway. The streets ain't that dangerous. Old people get mugged sometimes, but nobody would bother a couple of kids like us. All the houses have backyards, some have flower gardens, some have those cheap tin swimming pools, but we don't. The streets are lined with hedges and trees, so the smell of plants is strong on a cool night. But, man, the mosquitoes! I got bit a couple of times. So did Teddy.

Dangerous streets or not, we walked quick because it was dark and spooky. We were almost to the subway when Teddy couldn't control himself anymore. He just blurted out, "I'm in love, Caleb."

"With Julie?"

"I want to marry her."

Ted was only fifteen, so this was pretty silly. "Does she love you?" I asked.

"Yeah, she told me she loves me." I gave him a funny look because I was jealous. I was afraid he was going to ask about my nonexistent sex life and force me to start making up lies on the spot. I had no idea what to say.

"Congratulations," I said. I wish I had come up with something better than that. But that was enough for Teddy. He said he and I could be each other's best man in the future.

Down in the subway station, we had to wait forever. Teddy pulled a quarter out of his pocket and hurled it at a big rat running on the tracks. I was just glad it didn't run up on the platform. Sometimes late at night they get nervy and come right up onto the platform after half a candy bar or some trash.

When the train finally came, nobody was on the car, which was fine with me, except if a mugger got on, we would be the only ones to mug. With several people the mugger has to pick somebody plus worry about witnesses or kill everybody and get hunted down as a mass murderer. So I was a little nervous, but Teddy wasn't scared at all. But he was probably reliving his orgasm.

The train stopped, and a black man got on, dressed up for a date. I wasn't scared. I know which black people are trouble. I know from school. You can see the hatred in their eyes. This guy didn't hate anybody. He had probably just come from boning the hell out of his woman. He stayed on the train only one stop, then got off at Neptune Avenue. I teased Ted, the guy was too tired out from sex to walk six blocks home from his girlfriend's house. Ted thought that was funny.

A cop got on the next station. Typical! Two stops to go and now a cop. We could have been mugged six stations ago. But I was glad that hot black brother had got off the train. I mean, one black guy and two Jewish kids late at night on a train plus a cop. Automatically the black guy must feel like a criminal.

We finally got to Coney Island in one piece. It was a cool place to be at night. We walked past the roller coaster, then under the giant Wonder Wheel, and looked up into the pitch-black sky. Whoa, it was scary. Clouds were scurrying across the heavens, glowing white underneath from moonlight. On the boardwalk we could smell the ocean and hear it whispering. We walked south on the boardwalk past the kiddie park. God, how silly. Giant bumblebees smiling at you cockeyed.

Willy the Whale with a psychotic look on his face. Little polka-dot fire engines, carved clown faces around the top of the carousel. Even the kiddie park looked weird and crazy in the dark shadows.

Teddy wanted to walk on the beach, but I said no way. There might have been rats or dead birds in the sand. So we walked on the boardwalk past the new Coney Island to the old Coney Island from decades ago. The dead rides nobody goes on anymore.

We went under the old parachute drop and looked up until we got terrified. Then we played hide-and-seek by the old broken-down Wild Mouse. But I heard some dogs barking and got scared hiding by myself. So we sat under the raggedy papier-mâché demons of the abandoned House of Horrors. That was *totally* scary. They actually looked dead and ancient. Ghosts of ghosts, ghosts of devils.

"You balled Julie tonight, didn't you?" I said. I blurted it out to pretend I wasn't jealous. Honestly, I didn't want to hear about it.

Teddy stretched out his legs in a sensual way and told me how he and Julie went to the movies that night like always. When the man and woman were humping up on the screen, Julie started touching his nuts. "She opened my fly, and my joint popped out like a Pop-Tart," Ted said. Ted wanted to leave right then, but bossy Julie said no, let's finish watching.

So after the movie they got in a taxi, and Julie told the driver to take them to Brooklyn Tech. "We got nude and ran under the sprinklers on the football field. Julie raised her arms and let the water run down her breasts. 'You thirsty?' she asked. 'Yeah,' I said, and she let me suck cold water off her nipples like she was breast-feeding me."

"Pretty hot, little brother," I said.

"Then we went behind the scoreboard where no one would see, and I laid her."

"Did you like it?"

"Hell, yes. Ten minutes of heavenly vagina. Then we kissed, and I felt her up."

Right then I started to feel sad.

"Pussy is pretty sweet," I lied. I never much liked it myself.

"I can't wait to get some more."

Greedy fuck, I thought. I got a little pissed. "Didn't you try to get hard again?" I asked.

"No."

"Didn't you tell her to rub it? You can get hard and do it twice."

"I figured once was it."

"You didn't know because you're a kid."

"Next time I'll try that. But Caleb, I *love* her." Ted shook his head like he was howling. "I want to marry her."

Listening to this, I felt sick and sad. I didn't speak for a while. Then I started to talk about my old girlfriend Laurie, who hates me now, but I ended up bitching about Poppy. Ted sat there playing with his shoestrings while I bitched on and on.

There was one day — it was after my mom had divorced my dad and moved to Israel. Poppy took me for a drive to buy new shoes for school. But first he had to stop by the Court Street Social Club. "Just a few minutes," he said, but he was gone for an hour while I waited in the car. When he came back, he smiled like I was a *patza* for just sitting in the car.

We drove on the interstate up past Riverdale. Poppy forgot about my shoes, and I was too pissed to say anything. He just drove along the parkway for miles; then he pulled over on the soft shoulder and stopped the car.

"I met your mother up here, Caleb. She went to school in this town."

I thought Poppy had got drunk in the social club. But I didn't smell any liquor.

"What a fucking waste," he mumbled. I didn't know if he was talking to himself or me.

"So what ever happened to your girlfriend?" Poppy said. "You're not seeing any girls?"

I used to be straight. I had a girlfriend once, but she threw me out of her life.

"I'm seeing a girl," I lied.

"A boy your age needs a little pussy. Not all the time. Just a little so you don't turn into a fag."

That word *fag* — usually I pay no attention to it, but coming out of my father's mouth, it paralyzed me.

"Are you a fag, Caleb?"

"No, Poppy."

"Liar!" he said. I cried out, and Poppy shoved me up against the car window.

183

"No wonder you turned out queer with a bitch for a mother like you had."

Poppy grabbed at my hair. He caught a few strands in his fingers and pulled. It was hippie-long then, not short like it is now. I'm blond like my mother.

"Cut it out, Poppy," I cried.

"I never told you your mother was a junkie, did I? Yes. She was drinking and popping pills when she was pregnant with you. That's why you're a fag, Caleb. Side effects."

He was lying. Mom smoked pot, that's all.

"What a life," he went on. "The dumbest Jew in America I got for a son. You go to school with niggers and spics. It's your mother's revenge on me. A fag son." He pointed at me. "You're her *vengeance.*"

Teddy was patting my back. I could have told him right then. Poppy is right, I like *cock*! But I held it back. We stood up and walked along the boardwalk a ways. Three Spanish kids rode by on bicycles. It was very dark, and Teddy got spooked. So did I. So we ran back to the train station. We got back home after 3 o'clock.

The next day Poppy was at it at breakfast. Sweet as peppermint to Teddy, who was going to yeshiva and didn't cross his legs at the breakfast table like a queer. I didn't care. I had heard enough of it. I was bored.

I don't know how my dad figured out I was gay. Maybe when I was a kid I got hard watching Mr. Universe on television. Maybe I tried to goose my little brother in the bathtub.

184

I must have done *something,* because it didn't matter how hard I tried to hide it. Poppy knew I was queer, so I didn't rank in my house. Which is extremely rotten. My life sucked until I met my lover, Joe.

The day I met Joe started out as a typical fucked-up day. First I had a fight with Ted. It was his turn to go to market, but he wanted to go have sex with his girlfriend. That's not what he told Poppy, though. He made up a big lie, but Poppy favors Ted because he's going to yeshiva while I'll be lucky to get into community college. Poppy could kill me for that. "Can you see me on graduation day?" he said once at dinner, pointing his fork in my face. "The only Jewish parent sitting with all the *shvartzers.*"

So I had no chance of winning an argument that morning, but I started one anyway. "It's his turn, and he's *lying,*" I hollered.

"I'm not lying, Poppy," says Ted in his Boy Scout voice that I admit sounds lovely and soothing. "I promised to drive Julie to the eye doctor."

"Teddy has business with a *girl,* Caleb," decided Poppy. "You have nothing important to do."

Oh, yes, I did. I had to go into the city and find Bee-bee. But Poppy had made up his mind, so I had to go to market while Teddy got to go get laid.

I walked to the market with Poppy's grocery list in my back pocket, pissed as hell. Poppy wanted a two-week supply of fresh asparagus, celery, eggplant, and stuff for his heart diet. I headed right to the vegetable stand and made my way down the aisle, tossing green stuff into this grungy basket. I took my time at each bin, picking out the rotten ones because I was pissed.

When I got to the cucumber bin, I started having hallucinations. Those cukes turned into huge dicks. A hundred giant green cocks poking out at me. The light green tips looked like hungry puppy snouts — a bunch of puppies without eyes squirming to get to their mother's teats. I couldn't look away. I felt like laughing. Down the aisle the security guard was looking at me like it doesn't take ten minutes to pick out cucumbers. I started to feel like a criminal, so I walked away.

I had to stand in the cash register line forever. The clerk and this woman in a hairnet were arguing over expired coupons. Then the hairnet had to double-check the price of every item just to get even with the cashier for winning the argument. Meanwhile, Ted was having multiple orgasms about now, I guessed. Finally I paid for Poppy's vegetables and gave them the address to deliver. I got the hell out of that damn store.

Now I was free. And I was hot to find Bee-bee and get dusted. I had to get into Manhattan fast.

When I stepped off the D train at West Fourth Street, some winos were piled up in front of the train station. The piss smell was pretty strong. I got a good whiff, which made me mad. I walked over to Washington Square Park, but Bee-bee wasn't there, so I took a walk to look for him. I walked down Waverly Place, then up Bleecker to Christopher Street, and there in front of the Army & Navy store on the corner was

Bee-bee. He had his arm around this cute black kid who had a better ass than I do. At first Bee-bee ignored me. Then he grumbled "How you doin'?" and went on whispering to that other kid.

"I need some dust, Bee-bee," I said.

He said all he had was some good blotter acid. But Bee-bee's blotter was always fake, just little snips of sandpaper for you to lick on like a dope waiting for the high, so I said no, and he said look for him tomorrow and walked down the street with that black fairy with the beautiful ass.

The reason Bee-bee was blowing me off was I didn't let him fuck me when he tried to after getting me high on this great hash. He was pissed because he'd wasted some good drugs on a cockteaser.

I've known Bee-bee for years. When I was a kid, he sold me pot, and we became friends. He'd tighten me up with a free joint if I was broke or spot me a buck on a nickel. I knew he was messed up — he'd disappear for months, and I knew he was in jail. His teeth were all broken, and sometimes he stunk, but he was cool. Bee-bee gave me a brick of hash for my eighteenth birthday. It was the only present I cared about. I shook his hand for ten minutes. I just wouldn't let go. Bee-bee smiled and told me that brick wasn't my only present.

"What else?" I asked, still holding his hand.

He leaned over and whispered very sexily in my ear. "I'm gonna sit your butt right down on the Big Fat!"

I knew what he meant. I wanted to pull his pants down right in the park. I kept pulling on his shirt, saying, "Let's go,

Bee-bee." But he just got all cool and wiggled his shoulders and smiled and said he had to make some more money. Then some dope came up and asked for two measly joints. Why couldn't he clean Bee-bee out so I could go get my present?

Finally he sold all his loose joints, so we went over to his welfare hotel room. He turned on this cheap clock radio to the soul music station. I smoked my present in Bee-bee's cool hash pipe shaped like an African wood carving. While I was puffing away on his bed, he sat next to me and started massaging my crotch with his hands. Jesus in chains, was I stoned. And *horny*.

I didn't resist him feeling me up. My cock got stiff as a tree. I was proud of my steel-belted boner, even if it was for a man. Bee-bee shoved his hand down the back of my jeans, past my belt and my drawers, and tickled my butt crack with his finger. Then he got a finger in my asshole, and I jumped up.

"No, Bee-bee, I can't."

He stood up real slow like he was dancing, massaging his crotch with his hand. "Yes, you can, baby dawll." He rolled his hips around and gave his dick a shake. "I'mah throw some bone up your *be*-hind. And, girl, you gonna love it."

I ran out of that hotel like I was being chased by a madman. I walked to the train as fast as I could, cursing to myself in the street. Why were men always trying to hump me? What was I doing to lure on all these queers?

The next day I said hi to Bee-bee in the park, but he just waved me off. I *told* him I was sorry, but he called me a fucking little white cockteaser and a waste of good drugs. Shit!

Bee-bee was my best drug connection. Plus I liked him. I wondered about it all week, and that's why I was in such a hurry to find him that day Poppy made me go to market.

But he just blew me off when he saw me on Bleecker Street and walked away to throw some bone up into that beautiful black kid.

Now I was pissed, because I was looking for Bee-bee to tell him, yes, you can fuck me, and instead that black kid was gonna get it and the drugs too, plus his ass was way bigger than mine. And besides that, I really needed a hit of angel dust.

So I was walking back to the park to whip some *patza* at chess when I saw this man following me. First I got mad — I hated all homos since they never wanted to be just friends — they always have to fuck you. Joe followed me all the way to the park, kind of like a *patza,* to be honest. He checked me out a little, gave me a funny look, and went away. I figured he could tell I was straight and knew he didn't have a chance.

But he came back the next day, and we played chess. Joe stunk at chess, but he was tall and handsome, and his smile was beautiful. I wished he wore his hair in a cool black style, dreads or a cool fade, but he was old and he kept it plain and short. Still, I was flattered that he followed me the day before. My butt wasn't too skinny after all.

Joey and I started hanging out, and I finally made up my mind to get fucked. That's amazing, if you think about it. To let a man stick his dick up your *ass*? I mainly did it because Joe wanted me so bad. Looking at me, he narrowed his eyes, and he went *mmm* under his breath like I was a fox. I count six times I caught him looking at my butt. It was flattering.

The first time wasn't nothing, just this numb pounding. I felt a tight sensation deep inside me; then a flash of light went off inside my head. I was in agony. After a few times I started to like it, but mostly I loved the affection. Joey was my man, my lover. We went to baseball games. We ate pizza together. Joey had a lot of love to give.

It was such a pain holding up my male ego all the time. Just let it drop. Let it go. Stop fighting back for a few minutes while this man pussy-pounds the hell out of you. It felt great.

All these ideas come out of a trapdoor in my dreams. Crazy shit like, "Beat me, fuck me to death, please murder me."

Bam, bam, bam, bam. I groan in rhythm, first in fours. *Oh, oh, oh, oh.* Then twos. *Oh! bam. Oh! bam.* I have absolutely no power.

I like it on the bottom, deep in the pillows. Getting screwed on my back with my feet up in the air like a girl. The pinching feeling is good. Doggy-style is good too; it's more painful. I like sacrifice.

Then after, Joe is very gentle. He treats me like a jewel, kissing and hugging. When he falls asleep, I lay awake across his chest. Nice, cool air blowing up my busted-open crack. The hair on my forearm flittering in my lover's breath. My skin vibrates. I miss my man, boy.

Joe thought I was this clean-cut white kid from Carroll Gardens. I let him believe it, but after a few weeks I confessed how messed up I was. How I smoked angel dust and did so bad in school, my teachers put me in a special program for losers. Hell, I had it coming. In the first place I never fucking went. When I did go, I was busy fighting a war against three Puerto Rican kids, Randy, Hector, and Pedro. Randy called me "pussy pussy," and Hector and Pedro used to gang up and goose me in the bathroom until I brought a steak knife from home and pulled it on them. After that we got into a shouting match in the hallway almost every day. Plus I wasn't able to read that well.

I was ready to get rejected, but Joey just hugged me. And then he told me I wasn't a loser. It was hard being gay, Joe said, and only another gay person could understand the pressure I was under. My teachers and social workers and most of all my father didn't know squat. Joe promised to take over where Poppy failed me, since he had a kid himself and knew how to raise one right. This was a very exciting prospect. Joe gave me a part-time job and taught me computers. I didn't feel doomed anymore.

I liked making it with Joey, but I wanted other guys too, especially someone my age. Joe was kind of square, and having him act like my father all the time was a drag. He was always giving me the benefit of his experience. I had to hip him to everything new and cool. He never even heard of Pearl Jam! All he had were these ancient jazz records, plus the old bands from Woodstock.

Now that I was gay, in the park I was checking out the young basketball brothers and punk rockers and banjee boys and metalheads. I met these burnouts from upstate who liked Blues Traveler. I was looking for some hot young cock. I didn't call Joe all week long. I figured he'd get the message I was dumping him.

But after a few days I *had to* see Joey again. I panicked, thinking maybe he replaced me like Bee-bee did. So I called him up, and we talked like nothing had happened. He'd been busy all week at work designing campaign posters. He never even knew I had dumped him.

I tried it again after we had a fight because he wouldn't take me to Madison Square Garden when hot Michael Jordan came to town. I didn't care how much the tickets cost. But it still didn't work. I couldn't stay away. So we made up and stayed in, humping all weekend.

Joe felt guilty about being my lover since I was half his age, plus white. Twenty years ago, Joe said, our love affair would have broken every law on the books. He counted on three fingers — sodomy, race mixing, *and* statutory rape. I thought that was incredibly cool myself. But Joey got all moody and paranoid. Then worse, he got philosophical. "What if I had lived in the Old South?" he asked. He was drunk that particular night. "What if I was a Mennonite?"

As for me, I thought having a black lover who could buy me things and fuck me stupid and love me like his own son was the coolest thing in the whole fucking galaxy.

Once I saw Ted in Lefty's Pizza Shop smooching with his girlfriend. I pretended not to see him even though he saw me and waved. Another time I was walking home from school when I saw him and Julie holding hands coming in the other direction. I ducked around the corner before they saw me.

But once I had Joe, I wasn't scared of Ted anymore. I had my own life. Ted still thinks I just can't catch the rap with girls — but I don't care. I have somebody too. Now every time I see my kid brother yakking on his cordless phone with his girlfriend, I go right out and call up Joey on a pay phone.

Although I haven't called him the last two weeks.

It hasn't been much of a summer. Just very hot. Since Joe's kid came to town, I ain't been doing much of anything. Listening to music, cutting the grass. Smoking pot. Walking the dog. Going to work. And slipping around my neighborhood, checking out *other men.*

193

That's right. I'm cheating on my lover. I'm having an affair. I could say Joey and me have an open relationship, and I'm not doing anything wrong. It's not like we've been sanctified by God or something. But that's bull crap. Joe is my man, and I love him, and it's wrong to fuck other guys, but I'm doing it. Well, *he* said we couldn't see each other while his son is in town. I like feeling guilty — it's kind of an electric sensation. I like keeping secrets from Joey.

I'm having an affair with this Italian man named Pepe Iazetta. I love to say his name. That musical, rolling rhythm. I used to call him Mr. Iazetta. He painted our house when I was a kid and used to talk to me when Poppy wasn't looking. Pepe's old, and his body is covered with gray hair. He can't get his dick hard enough to stick it in me. That's all right. I still think of that as Joey's exclusive territory. Joey has hardly any body hair, but Pepe is like a big gray bear. I like to bury my face in that hair and wrap my arms around his big belly and tangle my legs up

194

with his. Pepe loves my long legs, just like Joe does. I used to think I was too skinny. But in sex it has advantages. My two men like slender guys, so it works out perfect. I'm starting to think I'm pretty hot. I *never* thought that before.

Pepe lives in Park Slope, about a half-mile walk from Carroll Gardens, where I live. I went over to see him twice last week. Well, Joe did say I couldn't see *him* for a while. I was walking down Bergen Street to visit my fat ol' Italian fuck buddy when I ran into this gang of girls standing on the corner. They all had those big female hairdos. Antigravity nets, I call them. Jenifer said hi first. She's lesbian, but nobody in the neighborhood knows but me. She's really sweet. I could almost make love to her, just because she's lesbian.

Jenifer was the first person I ever told I was gay. We stayed up late one night sniffing Special K at her house and talking about what it means to be queer in a straight world, and she bitched all over the nosybody straight people who can't just mind their business and let us live. That was before I met Joey, so I wasn't really gay yet. But I *felt* gay. That night with Jenifer was like sniffing laughing gas. I felt so light-headed, I thought my head would float away like a balloon. I love Jenifer. For that one night of honesty, I owe her for a lifetime. I almost wish somebody would jump her just so I could cut their nuts off and string them around their neck and save my lesbian sister's life.

Well, when I was going over to Pepe's house and I saw those girls, I waved to Jenifer, but I didn't stop to talk.

Because Laurie was there too. My old girlfriend. Oh, Laurie.

I don't have anything against Laurie personally, but I don't like seeing her, because it reminds me of when I used to be straight. I couldn't stand it. Jenifer told me that I was psychologically raped, and I agree with her. I was *forced* to fuck Laurie by society. Sex is so good with the right person and so bad with the wrong one. I mean, the *whole idea* is to have sex with somebody that *turns you on.* Right? Isn't that why God gave us eyes? To pick out who we want to have sex with?

Laurie was only fourteen when we started having sex. I was sixteen. She was madly in love with me. We'd lie in my bed naked, and she'd run her hands through my hair and tell me I was the most beautiful boy she'd ever seen and how much she loved my golden hair. Enough people seem to think I'm pretty hot, but I wouldn't choose to fuck myself, personally.

She didn't have any breasts when she was fourteen. Now she's got great big tits. They started growing when she turned fifteen, and the bigger they got, the more I hated to fuck her. She looked like a boy when I met her. But not when those tits started bulging out. Every time I saw them, they were bigger than the last time. Plus she used to wear her hair short. Now she's got this fancy feminine hairdo, and she wears eye blush and black lipstick. All the girls around here are trying to look like cover girls. Jenifer too.

Laurie looks at me now like I'm some curse out of her past. Who can blame her? You see, when those tits started booming and swelling and she sprouted hair on her pussy and her hips got big, I got mad. I wanted her to stay the way she was, useful to me and half boyish, with no makeup and short hair and tiny little tits like apples. And no brains either, at least not enough to see what a fraud I was. I was scared that when she turned into a woman, she would want the sex to last more than a minute, and she might ask me to eat her pussy, which I wasn't about to. And maybe she could tell the difference between a real French kiss and one where the man couldn't wait to get it over with.

I made fun of Laurie. I told her her tits were disgusting and too big and she needed to lose weight and go on a diet and stop eating whatever was making her tits grow too big. And I told her I didn't like fucking such a hairy pussy, she was too old, and I needed a new girlfriend with a fresh cunt. I told her I'd fuck anybody I wanted to, and I didn't care if she knew it. And when she came over with that antigravity hairdo, I just lost it. "Are you trying to lure on boys like a tramp?" I said.

Well, that was that. She wasn't only fourteen by this time. She was almost sixteen, and she wasn't such a vulnerable kid anymore. She smashed a Coke bottle across my bedpost and threw her pocketbook at me. I yelled back at her, but then she started screaming. Except she wasn't screaming at me. It was as if she had choked on a bone and was trying to scream it out of her throat. This was very purposeful screaming, like she was cleansing herself. I just stood there watching until she was finished. Then she stormed out of my house, and I never spoke to her again.

I think Laurie and me were both raped by society. Taken by force and abused. I'm just glad Laurie was smart enough to tell me to go to hell. If she had gone on loving me, I would have put her in a mental hospital. On purpose.

Pepe was glad to see me. Right away we got naked and into the shower. First we French-kissed under cool water. Then Pepe got down on his knees, pushed my legs apart, and gave me an *excellent* deep-throat blow job. Between the water and Pepe's mouth, I felt just fine. I thought to myself, *I want men all the time! I'm so fresh. Men kill for my butt.* I blew off a load that lasted twenty seconds, and my brain almost blew up.

Pepe turned off the water and dried me roughly with a terry bath towel. He acts very macho. After we were both dry, he fooled around and grabbed my wrists and wouldn't let go. You know, showing me that he was stronger than I am. I wrestled loose and gave him a shove. Then we walked into the living room and sat down on the sofa, both still naked.

I lied and said I had gone out to dinner with Joe. I didn't want Pepe getting any bright ideas about becoming my lover. "Is that the black guy?" he said, pretending he wasn't sure. Pepe wants me all to himself. So he grabs me roughly by the hand and lays his palm against mine. "You see this?" His face gets all serious. "*White* skin. White on white. It's all about *this.*" I listened and tried to look serious. Pepe was being such an asshole. "You're a white boy, Caleb. You're not supposed to sleep with black people." Black people. He wanted

198

to say "niggers," but he didn't dare. Not if he ever wanted to see me again. Pepe is just for sex. I love Joey.

When I thought about it, I was a little insulted. Pepe was saying that sleeping with Joe made me black or maybe I had a little black blood. Which is bullshit, because I guarantee you, if Pepe got the chance, he'd deep-throat Joe's juicy bone in a second.

I'm not black or anything, but when somebody says a racial thing right in front of me, it's confusing. It's like there are two worlds, one where racism is cool and one where racism sucks. All Pepe was saying was, "Well, I may be a faggot, but at least I'm white," which is a pretty degrading thing to think about yourself.

Pepe is mine. I didn't pay any attention to his racism. I laughed and moved close to him and stuck my tongue in his mouth. He just stood still with his mouth wide open while I sucked on his tongue. I could taste everything in there. Whiskey, steak and peppers, a cigar. I pulled back and looked at Pepe funny.

"Have you been eating pussy?" I asked.

"You caught me, Sherlock," he said.

I laughed and punched him in the shoulder. We always act dopey like that.

I stood up and got dressed while Pepe watched. He was still naked, sitting on the couch playing with himself. I took my time squiggling into my black Calvin Klein undershorts. Then I pulled on my jeans, my Nirvana T-shirt, and punk rock wristbands, though I was still barefoot. I walked over to Pep and lay down on the couch. He looked at me with this stupid expression he gets sometimes. Like he loves me or something. Who cares? I put my feet up in his lap and started tickling his dick with my toes. Pepe climbed on top of me, macho-style, and we French-kissed some more. "I got to go, Pep," I said after a bit. I walked over to the dining-room table to put on my socks and shoes. As I was pulling on my jacket, Pepe started talking.

"I could give you a job."

"In your painting business?"

"Yeah. You could drive one of my vans."

I was having a hard time getting my shoes on. I had just kicked them off before, and now I was too lazy to untie them and string them back up. It took a minute, but I shoved my heel down in there finally, and then I looked back up at Pepe. He looked at me like I was being rude.

"But then you'd be my boss, Pep," I said.

"What's wrong with that? I'm a nice boss."

"You're my hot fuck buddy, that's what you are."

"That too."

I checked for my wallet and my keys, because sometimes I forget them. Pepe was still staring at me with his silly fish look. *Give me a break,* I thought. "I already got a job," I said. "The only job I need is a *blow* job."

"You might reciprocate sometime, you know," he said.

I smiled and didn't say anything else. I just blew him a kiss and walked out.

The screen door slammed behind me as I stopped and took a deep breath on the stoop. *Oh, boy, that was good sex,* I thought. The sun was shining through the tree leaves pretty strongly, and I had to shade my eyes. It was comfortably warm now in the late afternoon.

I walked the long way home so I wouldn't run into those girls again. On the way I stopped at Lefty's Pizza and got a cheese-steak supersub. From there I ran home.

As soon as I got upstairs to my room, I put Silverchair on my stereo and plopped onto my bed. Now I was feeling truly fine. Chewing on that cheese steak and listening to my favorite band. Nothing the fuck to do. Two hot men in my life. I was basking in a romantic glow, feeling real conceited about Joey and Pepe. I just stretched out on my bed, kicked off my shoes, and relaxed. Just then my telephone rang. *Who the fuck is this?* I wondered. I didn't feel like talking to no goddamn body. I picked up the phone, and it was Derrick. Joe's son.

"Yo, bro', let's hang out," he said.

Why the hell was he calling me?

HIP-HOP

Derrick sat at the upstairs bar of Immensity, a discotheque on the east side of south Brooklyn. He stared curiously at a row of video screens — Technicolor razzle-dazzle and sex — his foot tapping the floor to the vibrating beat of hip-hop. Cat howls came from the crowded dance floor. He looked high above to a brass-barred balcony where the disc jockey, Air Female, waved wildly to the crowd below. In her tall aluminum hood and bra and blue sparkled goggles, Air was the newest star on the Brooklyn hip-hop scene. Spinning her turntables, fine-tuning her sound controls, she balanced rising tempo and volume, creating a skin-tingling wash of sound. She raised her arms like a mad witch, then with a finger released a stampede of rhythm. The crowd shouted its pleasure and began dancing.

Derrick bit on a chip of ice and turned on his barstool to watch the roomful of lithe young bodies undulating in long loops and panicky stomps. Some were cool, some in a frenzy, according to the ancient messages each one heard in the

Afro-Latin polyrhythms. The elephantine bass shook the floor beneath the dancers' feet. There were finger snaps and bravura hand claps, whistles and shouts. Bright faces stood out like images from dreams. The room was like a pot of boiling water circling from the heat, bubbling, bubbling, rising, and rising in excitement. Hip-hop energy crested and overflowed, rushing through Derrick's pores like a fleeing band of spirits.

Air Female finished her set. Quieter taped music came on, a blend of cool trumpet jazz and rap by a group named Digable Planets. Derrick turned back to the bar and drained his glass of cranberry juice and seltzer. He felt two damp palms slap down on his shoulders.

"Get up and dance, chump." It was Toast, his closest friend in the city.

"Later for you, bitch."

"Cincinnati is a farm town, huh, Chill? They got cows and chickens back home in Ohio, right? You country mo'fo'."

"I said later for you, bitch. I'm gonna take you up on the roof and throw your ass off, you keep messing with me."

"Chill out, Chiller."

A smooth-skinned girl, no older than seventeen, in a pink satin halter top and black shorts came up to the bar and squeezed her way between Toast and Derrick.

"Yo, Sophia, what you trying to do?" said Toast. "Get your own stool, woman."

"Introduce me to your friend," she said. "He looks like a *real* man. Not like you, Toast."

"Later for you."

"My name is Chill." Derrick extended his hand with minimal motion, trying to hide his attraction. Not successfully, though, as she smiled, as if to say "Got you," her eyes focused with insinuated power. Sophia's lipstick was aggressively red. Her shiny hair was drawn tight on her scalp, then tied into a frill of gemlike knots at the top. Her pink halter held back her breasts tenuously.

Toast ordered a vodka and tonic from the bartender. "With extra ice!" he shouted. When his drink came, he drained it in a gulp, then plucked an ice cube from his glass and shoved it down Sophia's shorts.

"Motherfucker!" She grabbed an ice cube from Derrick's drink, threw it at Toast, and walked away. Derrick's eyes followed her.

Toast touched Derrick on the shoulder. The next deejay, Tooti Booti, had started his set, and the music turned very loud again. Derrick leaned close while Toast shouted into his ear.

"You like Sophia?"

"She's brick, boy."

"You want some of that, right?"

Derrick smiled. The question was absurd, he thought.

"She's what you call a blow ho, dude. She be fiendin', boy. Freebase, white powder. Bitch do *anything* for the get-high. Give me twenty dollars, Derrick. We crack this bitch up, okay? Then we jam her up two for one. You down?"

Cheek in palm, Derrick studied the drunken, floating pupils of his friend since boyhood. He felt he was staring at someone asleep. Toast had grown wilder and angrier since last summer — his voice had a buzz saw in it now. Derrick had never done what Toast was proposing — two males in bed with one woman. The idea seemed queer. But the hot liquid sensation Sophia had aroused in his groin made the decision for him.

"I'm with it, bro." He slapped Toast's open palm, and the two of them followed Sophia out onto the dance floor.

The next morning Derrick woke up in Toast's bedroom with Sophia in his arms. Toast was still asleep, curled up on a floor rug with his hands clasped round his knees. When Derrick stirred, Sophia turned against his chest and pulled him closer to her.

"You awake, Sophia?"

"Don't move," she murmured, clearing her throat. Her rose-painted fingernails were pinched possessively into his rib cage. "You feel good. I'm keeping you."

The girl's breasts felt plump against his torso, and her thigh was snug against his genitals under the sheet. Derrick felt anxious. Gray memories of sex from the night before reminded him of how different he was from his father, who woke up in the morning next to men. Sophia shoved him and turned on her stomach, her breasts folded beneath her. He pulled back the sheet and looked up and down her naked body.

She had looked so beautiful undressing before him the night before — almost fat, her body curved like a dark vase, berry-black flesh escaping her underclothes. Yet when he lifted her, she was so light. Her bones could have been hollow, her big thighs filled with chiffon. He had carried her across the room, thrusting as he walked, studying her face as she orgasmed. Behind her, dizzy and drunk, was Toast on his knees, washing her buttocks with his tongue and snatching nervously at her pubic hair with his fingers.

Weird, Derrick thought, remembering male fingers playing a tremolo down below. The trace of a man's touch, even through the slipping skin of vagina, had sent him into a bull-like frenzy. He knocked Toast over backward, launching Sophia's butt into the bedroom door. "Yes!" she cried, licking his face all over. Below, Toast scrambled up on his knees and leaned with his nose to catch full on his face slap after slap from Sophia's flying bottom.

"New York is the land of freaks," Derrick murmured, inhaling wistfully as Sophia stretched out her legs and toes.

He glanced up and down the length of her body. Asleep again, she looked careless and supple. *Too comfortable,* thought Derrick. She seemed not at all afraid of him. Last night in his frenzy he had tried to dominate her. It hadn't worked. Instead she had absorbed his violence into a vacuum of feminine lust, consuming him, singing with pleasure. Derrick was afraid that somehow she had guessed that he had gay blood. It was his secret now, not just his father's. Could she tell from the way he fucked? From the way he kissed? Too tenderly? Was there a clue in his voice?

This is driving me crazy, he thought. He lay still, staring at the sunlight of dawn filtering through green cotton lace cur-

209

tains. He rested his head on Sophia's shoulder. After a long while, he fell asleep.

Stirring in the room awoke Derrick in the early afternoon. He opened his eyes in time to see Sophia kissing Toast on her way out the door. She smiled like a beckoning star, blew him a kiss, and closed the door behind her. Toast came over, jumped onto the bed, and began shaking Derrick by the shoulders.

"Wake up, Money. We got business to discuss, Homeboy."

"Get away from me, you freak. Licking that girl's behind. You wack, man."

Toast stood up and started shadowboxing the green curtains. "I can't help it, Chill. Sophia drives me crazy, boy." He jumped onto the floor and started doing jumping jacks. "Get up, Farm Boy. You in the city that never sleeps, my brother."

Derrick folded his arms behind his head on the pillow. Toast was searching for something under the bed.

"What's up, Toast, man?"

Toast pulled out a gym bag and groped about inside with his hands. He stood up, holding a black pistol in one hand and a large glassine bag of white powder in the other.

"What is that?" asked Derrick.

"Half kilo, bitch. Enough coke to keep the blow hos tripping on my dick all summer."

Derrick sat up in the bed. "What are you messing with, Toast?"

"Jump Street picked up my brother on a warrant, but they never found his stash. I got the money now, honey."

210

"What happens when your brother gets out of jail?"

"I'll just tell him Jump Street came and took it."

"Yeah, and what if he don't believe you?"

Toast wasn't listening. He fondled the barrel of the gun. Then he started dancing and waving the revolver in the air. "Jump Street better not fuck with me now, Jack. I'll kill a cop for Rodney King. Rodney King ain't had no gun. I got a gun. They killed that Spanish kid right in front of his own mother."

Derrick's face shriveled in confusion. "Toast, I'm going back to sleep for a little while, and then I'm splitting. You ain't getting me sent up to Sing Sing."

Toast was gone when Derrick awoke an hour later. The gun was gone too. The glassine bag was stuffed under his pillow. Derrick took a sniff and tossed the bag under the bed.

He had been dreaming about Sophia — about her belly button, exactly. Right away he wished she hadn't gone. The window was open, and a guttural sobbing came from the street. *Some wino with the DTs,* Derrick thought. Street sisters with high voices were cursing out some fool on the avenue. Toast lived in a failing tenement section of Brooklyn, a half mile from the Marcus Garvey Houses. So different from the two-story home Derrick lived in in Cincinnati or his father's Manhattan high-rise.

Pulling on his shorts, he recalled the day in second grade that Toast stood up on his desk and announced he would no longer answer to Donald Lipton "Tee." "I'm black like burnt

211

toast, so call me that." That day during lunch, playing ring-a-levio, the two of them became friends.

It was 2 o'clock in the afternoon. It disgusted Derrick that he was just getting up. For days he had been sleeping late, not exercising, drinking, running around Brooklyn with Toast. For the first time in his life, he had done cocaine. He hadn't talked to his father in a week. But he had come to New York to get his dad's attention, to try to grow up, to tell his father he wanted to move in with him. Why was he here instead?

It was Caleb's fault. Derrick had begun thinking of his father's lover by name rather than as "that white devil." He looked into his wallet and pulled out the slip of paper with Caleb's telephone number.

If it weren't for Caleb, he wouldn't be in Brooklyn now, Derrick thought. He wouldn't be fighting with his father or wasting his days getting high or having strange sex. Derrick pulled on his blue jeans and black tank top. He stuffed his socks into his pocket and pulled his Air Jordans over his bare feet.

When he went out into the hall, he saw Toast's grandmother dust-mopping the floor. She was a spindly, ancient woman with dark, ashy skin. Tilted on her head was a spiderlike, red-tinted wig that mocked glamour ferociously.

"Ma'am, do you know where Toast is?"

"How would I know where that asshole is? He keep bringing those hussies into my house."

The walls in the tenement house were cheap hollow plaster. Of course she had heard his ménage à trois last night. Derrick shook his head. The old woman hadn't stopped talking.

"...his father wasn't worth shit, and his mother ain't shit, and neither is he."

"I'm sorry about the noise, Mrs. Lipton. When Toast comes in, could you tell him to call me?"

"I will, honey." Mrs. Lipton had been Derrick's baby-sitter years ago, and his father always paid her generously — especially toward the end of the month, when the social security for Toast's dead father was running low. "How's your daddy doing? Is Joe all right?"

He's a faggot, Derrick thought. "He's fine," he answered politely.

"He's a nice man, your daddy. He does his best."

Derrick said good-bye and hurried out into the street. The sun hurt his eyes with its sudden brightness. On the corner was a pay phone. As he had guessed, there was a groaning wino lying on the sidewalk, eyelids fluttering, his red palms to the sun. Derrick stepped over the man into the phone booth and dialed the number on the slip of paper. His heart pumped hard as a soft, nervous voice answered.

"Who is it?"

"Your mother's worst nightmare, chump."

"Who is this?"

"This is Derrick. Remember me?"

"Oh. Joe's son. How's Joe?"

"Like you don't know."

The phone was silent for several seconds. "What do you mean by that?"

"You work for him, don't you?"

Caleb sounded frustrated and annoyed. "What do you want?"

"Yo, man, let's hang out."

After much cajoling, Caleb agreed to meet Derrick in front of his grandmother's house that evening. They walked past kids dancing in the water flow from an open fire hydrant, then through a playground. Girls ran laughing, screaming from boys. Not-so-young men fired basketballs at bent non-regulation rims. Derrick assumed Caleb was excited by heterosexuals jumping around in cutoff sweatpants.

"You ever been in this part of Brooklyn?" Derrick asked.

"Never," said Caleb.

"You weren't curious? This is where my father grew up."

"Joe never really mentioned this place."

"My grandmother has lived here for thirty years. My dad went to junior high school over there." Derrick pointed to an orange brick building surrounded by a ten-foot-high metal fence. Behind the fence a quartet of boys turned somersaults on a stained, springless mattress.

"It's different from where I live."

"You mean the all-white section, right?"

"No. There's some black people in my neighborhood. Puerto Ricans too."

"Do you know that dude with the Southern accent?"

"Southern accent?"

"He's gray like you. He sells drugs. He hangs out with my father."

"Oh. Macon Summerscale. No, I never met him."

214

"Macon Summerscale?"

"Your father helped him. I think he saved his life or something."

Derrick's heart drummed in his chest. He had never talked to a homosexual other than his father, and even then he had never talked *about* it. He wanted to shout out the word — *queer*! It felt daring to talk, without hate or laughter, about two men having sex. Yes, the daring, the boldness of talking about it, was tempting to Derrick. It felt almost like lust.

He was still angry at this skinny, bothersome gay boy with blond hair curling prettily behind his ears, his thin nose, and lips twisted warily. But more now, Derrick felt a need for answers. What could Caleb tell him about the invisible wonderland in which his father floated like a ghost? When he telephoned Caleb, Derrick had feared he might punch the white boy the moment he saw him. He didn't feel that now. His father was still hiding from him behind an insultingly transparent facade. The only person he could talk to about it was this white devil.

"Listen. I know you a homo. I know about you and my father."

Caleb stared at him for a moment. "So?" he said defensively.

"So let's talk about it."

Caleb shrugged. "What do you want to know?"

The two boys walked through the projects and down along the Brooklyn waterfront. Derrick asked questions, many of

215

them silly, thought Caleb. But gladly he told the old gay stories — tales of the homo tribe — of coming out and how it all felt. Things he had read in books, things he had told to doctors, obvious things. Stories he wished he could tell to his own kid brother.

"But just because you want something, that don't mean you supposed to get it."

"Why not?" asked Caleb.

"Man, look. Imagine I'm walking down Court Street, and I see this brick babe with big tits. Man, I want to fuck her right in the street. But if she don't dig me..." Derrick smiled brazenly. "I know it's beyond imagination, but just pretend hypothetically she doesn't want me. Too bad for me. But so what?"

"But that's not mutual desire."

"That's not the point. What I'm saying is, nobody gets to fuck whoever they want. Some girlie is digging me, she better be brick, boy. She gots to have a big ass too, or she's out of luck. Say she wants a movie star. Or a billionaire. Or another woman. So she can't have it. Tough. That's life."

Caleb looked at him puzzledly. "You're crazy," he said. "I think people *should* get what they want."

It was growing dark. They were headed toward Immensity. Caleb had been there before on the nights when heavy metal bands played. But Friday night was hip-hop night. Mistress G, Air Female, and the famous reggae band One World Two Spirits were performing. The club would be crowded. Derrick asked Caleb if he was nervous about going.

216

"Why should I be nervous?"

"There won't be any gray dudes there except you."

"What is a gray dude?"

Derrick sucked his teeth. "It's an expression black people use for white people. You know, gray dudes. White people." He waved his hands in mock exasperation. Caleb shook his head, and Derrick smiled.

"There'll be lots of fine women."

Caleb looked to the ground.

"Do you like to fuck girls?" asked Derrick.

"Yes." Caleb's voice rose sharply in an ambiguous inflection.

"You ever balled a black chick?"

"No. I would like to, though."

"But you afraid to ask, right?"

"No. The girls in my neighborhood keep me happy." Caleb looked away from Derrick. "It doesn't make a difference what color."

"What about that babe at Vector Media, Dolores? Can't you rap to her?"

"Are you kidding? She must be thirty years old."

Derrick's eyes narrowed. His father was somewhere near forty, but that hadn't stopped Caleb. The gay boy was lying to him, he concluded. Derrick sucked his teeth.

"You afraid of women, man. I bet you'd have a nervous breakdown if you saw pussy up close."

Caleb didn't answer. He just walked along silently, looking off into the shadows and tall weeds that lined the deserted street. His composure made Derrick angry.

217

"You have to come on *powerful* with bitches. I wolf-pack the girlies. I walk right up and start rapping. 'I like your body, baby. I'm taking you home, sister.' " Derrick picked up a rock and hurled it at a water rat scurrying along the base panels of an empty warehouse. "I know I'm getting me some pussy tonight. I'mah *jam* it up too." He stomped his foot in the gravel path.

"How come you talk so bad about women?" asked Caleb.

"What do you know about it?"

"You sound like you hate them. I think *you're* afraid."

"Is that because down inside you're really a bitch?"

Caleb didn't answer. Derrick's ferocious sexism insulted him — but he was also excited by it and guiltily sympathetic. He had been as bad, even worse with the girls he had slept with. In his life Caleb had played both parts, the ruthless male and the woman hoarding her secrets of power. He remembered the night Derrick's father had taken his virginity. For days after he felt ashamed of his feminine wants. But now he freely mimicked the woman's way with men every bit as rough as Derrick. Sexy tricks in bed with his legs, wishbone-splayed and rope-grappling, the way the Park Slope girls had taught him as they tried futilely to please him.

The secrets worked like a wizard's wand on all the men he had ever been with. How they followed him, how they waited for him, like puppy dogs after just a sniff. *I can get anything I want,* he thought, feeling bold and calmer now. He decided that Derrick was naive when it came to sex.

"Bump you," said Derrick. "You don't know the first thing about pussy."

Both boys were flushed with their bubbling young hormones, erect in their dungarees as they walked in the damp night. Both were aroused, Caleb with preposterous fantasies about son and father. Making love with Derrick; would it be like carrying Joseph's child? And a ménage à trois with both of them — father and son taking turns. *Oh, goodness!* Caleb thought.

And Derrick — hot to find Sophia and fire off the charge he had ignited in himself by shouting dirty words in the dark — he too was unbearably aroused. As he yelled into the ear of a boy his age who slept with men, Derrick decided he would hold nothing back tonight.

There was a palpably nervous edge to the crowd at Immensity that Friday night. The evening before, just before closing, two Dominican men had been murdered by gunfire in front of the club. The police had returned to the club earlier tonight, asking questions and randomly searching for weapons. Now everyone was certain there were undercover cops among the crowd.

"Yo man, don't say nothin'," Toast said when Derrick and Caleb arrived. "Don't say shit. Jump Street is hangin' in plain clothes, man."

"What's going on?" asked Derrick.

"They fired up these two Dominican dudes last night. Over a bitch, you believe that? I'll smoke a stupid motherfucker for some money, but I ain't gonna kill for pussy."

Derrick's eyes quickly searched the dance floor. A small crowd of women were standing in front of the ladies' room, and he thought he saw Sophia among them. He flinched as Toast leaned close and whispered in his ear.

"Yo, who's the gray dude, man?"

Derrick glanced at Caleb, who was standing by a post with his hands in his pockets, bobbing his head to the deafening reggae. One World Two Spirits was onstage.

"That's my stepbrother or something."

"You kidding?"

"Of course. He works for my father."

"He's a cool gray dude, huh? He likes to hang with the people of color?" Toast eyed Caleb again. "That's okay, man," he muttered whimsically. "Gray cats can be cool sometime."

A man in a sweat suit and a woman in denim shorts, holding hands, pushed their way past Derrick and Toast. "If you got anything, get rid of it," the man whispered. "The police definitely in here."

"Thanks, bro," said Toast.

"Yeah, thanks, man," said Derrick.

"I wish I had my thirty-eight," said Toast. "I'd have me some smoked pig for dinner, boy."

"Will you stop talking stupid, Toast?"

"They doin' illegal searches and seizures, man. I don't play that shit. They better show me some mo'fucking probable cause before they search me, godmotherfuckdamnit."

Toast was slurring his words. Derrick could tell that he was already stoned, probably on cocaine mixed with another chemical to slow him down.

"You seen Sophia?" Derrick asked.

"First thing on your mind, huh, Homeboy? Listen, man, I'm setting up an instant replay for later. You down, Derrick?"

221

"Yeah. Is she here?"

"She's over by the bar. See her?"

Derrick grabbed his crotch. "Mmm. I can't wait for some more of that." He hopped on his toes excitedly. "I'm ready to *jam it*!" he exclaimed. He turned around, still holding his crotch, and looked at Caleb, who seemed oblivious. "Chill out, Caleb. Get yourself a drink, enjoy the music."

"What's up, my man? My name is Toast."

"I'm Caleb."

"He wants to ball a black chick," said Derrick. "He ain't never had none."

"Oh, you cuckoo for Cocoa Puffs, huh?"

Caleb grinned. "Is Robin Givens here?"

The two black boys laughed. "No, she ain't here, man," said Derrick.

"Robin Givens! He be driving into trees over that babe."

"I'mah set you up, Caleb, all right?" said Derrick. "You just be cool. I'mah get you some."

Toast put his arm around Caleb's shoulder. "Some of those Puerto Rican chicks are beautiful too, Caleb. Yo, Derrick, you got to meet this Latino babe named Dominica. Brick, boy!" He turned back to Caleb. "Listen, man, you got a credit card?"

The Chinese boys came to the club most Friday nights. There were six of them, three pairs of cousins, and every weekend they brought different girls. They came for the music, and they stayed quietly among themselves. There were rumors that they bought and sold cocaine, and Derrick noticed that the youngest of the six kept disappearing into the bath-room. He grabbed Toast by the shoulder and pulled him close.

"What about those Chinese dudes?"

"What about them?"

"Dump your brother's blow on them. Tell them they can take it back to Chinatown and cash out."

"They don't come from Chinatown. The mo'fuckers hang up on Neptune Avenue. I see them all the time."

"I don't give a damn where they live, motherfucker. Why don't you sell them the blow?"

"I'mah cook that shit, Derrick. They ain't gonna give me what it's worth."

"No, no, no. Dump it on these Chinese cats and cash out in one shot."

"What do you think of that, Caleb?"

"I wouldn't try to sell rock around here. It's too hot," Caleb answered.

Derrick looked at him in surprise. Now the gay boy thought he was street cool and bad too.

"I was gonna cook that shit. Make me some real money."

"No, no. If you cook it, you gonna smoke it all up. Then you'll start acting stupid. And your stupid ass is stupid enough already."

"What's wrong with you, Derrick?"

"I ain't running with no crack dealer, man. You sell the coke to those Chinese cats, and we can split." Derrick turned away and muttered to himself. "Nigga don't know how to cook a can of soup, talking about he gonna cook some crack."

"I think it's too hot," offered Caleb. "You might get caught, after that shooting."

"I think you right, Caleb. Jump Street is hangin'." Toast put his hand to his chin and stood pensively for a moment. "Yeah, Caleb, I'm digging what you saying, man. You make a lot of sense."

Derrick grabbed Toast heavily by the shoulder. "I'm going to set it up, all right?"

"Okay, Chill, you set it up. A hundred bucks a ball. Five balls, five hundred dollars. And don't take no shit from those Chinese motherfuckers. They come into *my* territory thinking they bad with their war haircuts and shit."

Derrick shook his head mockingly and walked over to the bar, where Sophia was sipping a cocktail and talking to an older woman, in her middle twenties, in a glittery green pantsuit.

"Hi, Derrick," said Sophia. "This is my friend Jocelyn."

"Hello, sweetness. You look real nice in that suit."

"Are you a friend of Toast?" asked Jocelyn.

"Word up. We go way back."

"Yeah, but he's not crazy like Toast is," said Sophia.

"Listen, Sophia. We're going to sell some blow to those Chinese dudes over there. Could you come with me to set it up?"

Sophia looked at him suspiciously and then stood up. "Josie, we'll be back in just a minute."

Derrick led Sophia by the waist across the dance floor, whispering the deal in her ear. The six Chinese boys were crowded by the wall. Two of them were laughing. One wore pink-framed mirrored sunglasses. *Too silly,* Derrick thought. He decided to approach the tallest, quietest boy, whose hair was cut conservatively. The others wore an assortment of spikes, white streaks, and ponytails.

The tall boy's name was Frankie. His heavyset cousin was named Ho. Derrick briskly made the offer, and Sophia stepped in and whispered the price. Frankie and Ho seemed interested, both in the cocaine and in Sophia.

The deal seemed agreed to. Derrick turned and peered across the room. Through the dancers he saw Caleb and Toast standing shoulder-to-shoulder, whispering in each other's ear. He turned back to Ho.

"You see that white guy over there?"

"What about him?" asked Frankie.

"He told me he wants to blow you. He said he'd give you money. He got a MasterCard, he take you out to dinner, and then you two can have sex."

"You joking?"

"He gave me a ten-dollar tip to tell you. Shit, I don't give a damn."

"That pale-face nigger-mother motherfucker must be crazy," said Frankie.

"He told me to tell you he was good. He wants to polish your knob, man. Dude said you'd need sunglasses to take a piss." Derrick looked at the cousin in the flashback Foster Grants and laughed. "Like this dude. He's already equipped."

"Why is he asking me?"

225

"That's what I said!"

Sophia pulled Derrick away and whispered into his ear. "Is that true?"

"I'm just playing," he whispered back.

"That's not funny, Derrick."

"Okay, brother, listen," Frankie said. "Two things. As for the coke, meet us out front at 3 o'clock. I don't got the money on me now. As for your faggot friend, I'm going to show him something."

Frankie and Ho, with Sophia and Derrick following, pushed through the crowd over to Toast and Caleb.

"What's up, brothers?" asked Toast.

"We can do some business," said Frankie. He glanced angrily at Caleb. "Meet us out front at 3 o'clock. We'll try it, and if it's good, we'll take five balls for five hundred dollars."

"Cool. Three o'clock. Got you."

"Is the skinny faggot going to be there?" Frankie looked at Caleb.

"There's going to be three of us there," said Derrick.

"Two men and a little chicken," said Frankie.

Caleb flinched. In the noisy crowd, under the flashing lights, he realized that Frankie was insulting him. He was too caught up in the techno and hip-hop to take it. He got nervous, which he didn't like, and he blamed that on Frankie too, and then he became angry. He spoke before he could think.

"Watch your mouth!"

"You're the one with the mouth," answered Frankie. "I can't believe your fucking nerve."

"Well, maybe if you had something besides dog shit inside your skull!"

"Be cool, people," said Toast. "What is this shit?"

Frankie looked at Toast, his eyes flaming up a touch. "I want a bonus. A little sweetener. A blow job for me and my cousin by the skinny little chicken here. In public, in front of everybody on the street." He turned to Caleb. "I want to piss down his throat."

Caleb shoved Frankie's shoulder. "You better shut your mouth, you stupid fucking idiot," he screamed.

"Don't touch me again, homo."

Sophia moved next to Caleb and put her arm on his waist, pressing fingers into his hips. She glowered at Frankie. Caleb shoved Frankie again harder, and Derrick stepped between them. The floor security guard, a short, very muscular man, had seen the argument brewing and was pushing his way rudely through the crowd.

"Out! Take it outside. All you assholes get out now!"

"Homeboy, we got it under control, man," said Toast. "It was just a small misunderstanding."

The bouncer pointed toward the door aggressively. "Are you crazy? We already had two punks shot in here last night, and you want to start more trouble?"

"It's over now, brother," said Derrick.

"Get the fuck out!"

Sophia sucked her teeth. "Oh, Derrick! You made me waste ten dollars to get in here."

"I don't have time for this, people," said the bouncer. "Follow me to the door, please. Right now." Frankie, his

227

cousin, Toast, Derrick, Caleb, and Sophia formed a line and followed the security guard through the crowd. The other Chinese saw Frankie and Ho and followed.

"You staying?" Sophia called to Jocelyn as they passed by the bar.

"What for?" Jocelyn said.

"Come on then, girl."

Out in front of the club, Derrick tried to clear up the confusion before a fight started. "No, no. I made it up, Frankie. I had to test this dude to see if he was a punk or not. I had to know whether we could run with him. You understand, right?"

"That wasn't funny, man," said Frankie, turning to Caleb. "Sorry to jump on you. He said some freaky shit about you."

"Yo, man, what about the blow?" asked Toast.

"Meet us up this street at 3 o'clock," said Ho. It was about 11:30.

"I'm down, dude."

Frankie shook Toast's and Caleb's hands, gave Derrick a dirty look, and then he and his cousins walked off.

"That was cold, Chill," said Toast.

"Yeah," said Caleb, looking evasively, wonderingly at Derrick.

"*Yeah,* Derrick," said Sophia. "You brought your friend to the club and then set him up like that."

"I wanted to see how he would react. I knew Caleb could take care of himself."

228

"Word up. You stood right up to the motherfucker, Caleb. You a badass white boy, huh?" Caleb and Toast slapped palms.

"So what are we going to do now?" asked Jocelyn. "Now that Derrick got us kicked out of the club."

There was a short, loud argument, with Sophia repeatedly shoving Derrick and blaming him for wasting her money.

"Why don't all of you come over to my place?" said Jocelyn. "It's not far. I live on Willoughby Street."

"That's cool. We have to anyway. That's where I stashed the blow," said Toast.

"Toast, don't tell me you left that mess at my house," said Jocelyn.

The icy bass groove and whispered, demented poetry of Tooti Booti's "Honk If You Eat Pussy" made Derrick narrow his brow. So late at night he could feel the cocaine in his fingertips. He looked around Jocelyn's living room, eyeing nude bodies. An engine revved up in his belly. The lights were dimmer than candles, and the speakers had turned into tiny square cartoon androids, speaking terrible things to him. The song came to an end with a cacophony of car horns.

Derrick's penis was numb with hardness. He watched it bob about in the air like a balloon on a tether. Across the room Sophia lay on the carpet with her eyes closed. Caleb, wide-eyed from drugs, was stretched out on the floor. Derrick looked back at himself. Then he looked thoughtfully at Caleb, then at Toast, who was on the sofa making love with Jocelyn.

Derrick was searching for gay desire, opening himself to its possibility. If he waited long enough, would it come out of its hiding place? What might activate the gene? Was he even a little queer?

Naked on the floor, Caleb looked hopeless and immobile, vanquished by coke. Across on the sofa Toast's hips wiggled fluidly. Derrick watched his thigh muscles flex and relax, strain and relax. He glanced again at Caleb, whose skin looked hazy and dark in the minimal light.

I don't feel a thing, he thought. *I don't want to have sex with no goddamn man.*

Sophia inhaled a line of cocaine along the edge of the coffee table. Derrick stood up unsteadily and followed his floating penis across the room. He reached out his hand. She looked up and giggled.

"Stand up for a second," he said, wriggling an invitation with his fingers. Sophia brushed the grains of coke from her nostrils, took his hand, and tried to rise from the carpet.

Before she could stand, Derrick lifted her in a swoop. She felt weightless as he held her airborne, his hands around her waist. She stretched out her legs like a dancer as Derrick lowered her gently onto his penis. They kissed. The taste of cocaine was on her tongue.

"I'm going to eat you up, Chiller," she said. "Won't be nothing left of you."

She dug her heels into his buttocks. Derrick slipped a bit, regained his balance. "Hold my back," she said coolly. Then she relaxed into his hands, swinging her legs up onto his shoulders. Delighted, Derrick held her in his palms — as if he were serving a waiter's tray of baked sweets. Inside he felt

231

himself trapped tight in a pocket of flesh. Sophia made fine adjustments, rolling her thighs against his chest with finesse. Then she began to sing "Oh-oh-oh" in a throaty, descending melody, her feet pattering on his shoulders. Her red lips turned inward, and her nose twitched.

Then came the long, swooping alto wail. Quaking thighs and a mushy flood that tickled. The floor was wet, and Derrick slipped, catching Sophia before she fell, then laying her gracefully on the carpet. She curled up her legs like an embryo. Derrick laid his twitching penis on top of her labia, and without a touch his sperm flooded out, dripping down her creased waist, pooling in her navel.

He turned away and gasped for breath until his heart stopped pounding. Sophia turned to touch Caleb with a finger, rocking her knees apart slowly.

Sophia's brain radiated with a coke high. She wanted two boys; that was her thing lately, and besides she was curious about the gray one — Caleb? — who had caught her eye when he faced up to Frankie. Skinny, screaming like a seagull. Why was he hanging with Derrick? All she knew was that his hips, where she touched, were padded with baby fat, not iron like Derrick's. Nice. More like a girl.

Caleb wanted only to lie still and enjoy the drugs and music, but Sophia kept tickling his ear. "Do it, Caleb," someone said. He looked up and saw in the dimness a blurry frown on a black face. What was Joe doing here? He looked awfully young. "Do it, do it." Shadow veils dropped down along the wall. Joey? How can that be? It couldn't be his lover. It was mean Derrick, the straight asshole, telling him what to do.

Sophia took his penis in her hand. Caleb glanced hotly at Derrick, then fell forward and rubbed around in Derrick's sperm, still warm and slick on her stomach.

It looked to Derrick as if the gay boy was trying to crawl inside of Sophia. His feet flipped about on the floor, and his head kept bumping the wall behind her. A gay man with a woman. Dizzy from coke, Derrick dreamed he was watching his own conception. Sophia let out a sigh. A convincing one, thought Derrick, surprised. Sophia sighed again.

"She's diggin' you, Caleb," he said, almost tenderly.

Toast and Jocelyn were sitting up arm in arm, smiling. "Right on, Caleb," Toast called out, with an unfamiliar clearness in his voice. His hand was cupped over his penis, which was very large and looked to be coated with caramel. Jocelyn came across and began touching Sophia's breasts. The two women kissed. Derrick leapt vigorously to his feet.

"I'm going to take a shower."

"Caleb, come here," said Toast once Derrick had left the room. He took his hand away from himself. "Come here, baby."

Caleb didn't remember moving, but somehow he got into Toast's arms, and they were kissing. Tongue, a long wad

233

wiping dry lips, tickling his tonsils, stuffing his throat until he coughed.

"Sorry," said Toast. Caleb looked at him dizzily, leaned over, and began to swab the fat caramel cock with his mouth.

It was the largest and sweetest he had ever tasted. Outside it was spongy, balloonlike and soft. Underneath, stiff muscle resisted Caleb's tongue. A fingertip was at his rectum, brushing gently at first. He thought he felt fingerprints. Then pulling at hairs, spinning them as if to thread a needle. His jowls were overstuffed. The finger punched in and out, up to the knuckle. His mouth worked hard, a lifetime of fantasies to be fulfilled with this one brief chance. Quickly. Caleb heard the shower water still running, but Derrick would be back soon.

It turned into a bumpy ride as Toast shook and heaved upward. Caleb wrestled the wagging thing, his head following every snap and turn to keep from gagging, like a mongoose outguessing a snake.

Toast reached down between the sofa cushions and pulled out a condom package. He tore the corner of the packet, and Caleb sat up.

"I'd love to, but I can't."

"That's a real shame."

"Don't you like it oral?"

"Cool," said Toast.

Caleb looked up with a start. Derrick was behind the sofa staring at him, wrapped in a towel, his black eyes surreally bright in the candlelike dimness.

"Did he see us?" Caleb and Toast asked each other with just their eyes.

It was 2:30. They had thirty minutes to get back to Immensity and meet Frankie. Caleb and Toast took hurried turns in the shower while Sophia and Jocelyn sat in pajama tops on the sofa, talking in dreamy voices, laughing at the scurrying nude males as they shared a Thai stick. They also shared Jocelyn's pink cotton bunny slippers. One bunny flop, on Jocelyn's right foot, nuzzled the other on Sophia's left. Sophia asked Jocelyn's slipper if it wanted a sip of vodka.

"Hurry up, Toast," Derrick shouted.

Toast wriggled into his jeans, then stood picking out his hair in front of the hall mirror. Caleb was next to him, whispering in his ear. The two of them exchanged a private laugh.

"They ain't going to wait, man," said Derrick. "Later for your hair. Let's go."

"I'm hurrying, Chiller." Toast came into the living room with Caleb right behind. He looked into the closet and retrieved from the pocket of a yellow raincoat a glassine bag filled with small manila packets.

"I gotta sit here waiting for two bitches to put on their makeup," muttered Derrick. "I'm the only man here."

The girls laughed at this. Caleb laughed also.

"Chill out, Derrick," he said.

"Did you say something, Caleb?" Derrick asked coldly.

"Ooh!" cried the women in unison. Both bunny flops danced and shook their pink noses at Derrick. Caleb waited until the girls stopped giggling.

"Yeah, I said calm down."

Toast sat on the edge of the coffee table, tying his sneakers. "That's right, Derrick. Relax. Put this in your pocket." Toast handed him a manila packet. Caleb watched as Derrick stuffed it into his cuffs. "Those cats can wait a couple of minutes. You know they want this blow." Toast stuffed the glassine bag, short by two grams, down under the lip of his sneaker.

"Man, I ain't walking all the way down there for nothing," said Derrick.

"Ah, take a pill, Chiller," said Caleb, gesturing boldly with both arms.

"You tell him, Caleb," said Sophia.

Toast stood up and reached around to feel behind his back. He gave his belt a shake. "I'm ready. Okay, sweet sisters, we'll be back in a little bit."

And the three boys crowded through the front door and bounded noisily down the stairs and out into the street.

The morning had turned chilly. Toast and Caleb whispered as they walked. Derrick walked close to the curb, ignoring them and thinking. The passing of a car in the street, soft thumping over cobble, made him shiver. The sound reminded him of driving with his father years ago over Brooklyn streets late at night, coming from his grandmother's, feeling safe in

236

the car. Unlike the night streetwalkers — syrup-thick darkness touching their skin — who were exposed to unknown dangers.

A tugboat on the nearby river hooted dispiritedly. Derrick could almost feel the great weight of some lazy tanker being towed with difficulty up the river. He filled his lungs with moist air blowing east from the river, scented with oil engine ash and chemicals. The tug sounded again.

They were hurrying to cover the ten city blocks to the disco. They would probably be late, thought Derrick. Frankie wouldn't be there. He was wasting his time. And he didn't want to go back to Jocelyn's. He didn't like Sophia anymore — only because she fucked Caleb, although Derrick had made it happen by daring him to do it. And the way Caleb had eyed him right after, looking smug and accomplished. He was on the opposite side of Toast now. The two of them had been talking since Jocelyn's. Derrick hadn't spoken a word. He skipped around Toast to Caleb's shoulder.

"I know why you're scared of me," he said.

"I'm not scared of you," Caleb answered.

"*O*-kay. If you say so." Derrick grinned comfortably.

"I haven't forgotten what you did at the disco with Frankie."

"Yeah, that was wrong, Chill," said Toast. "People could have got hurt."

"It was a test." Derrick eyed Caleb's profile. "You surprised me. I thought you were a punk."

"Just because I'm gay?" Caleb's voice was acidic.

"I'm checking you out. That's what this whole night is about."

"I don't have to meet your approval."

"Yes, you do, motherfucker."

"Sophia liked me more than you."

Derrick laughed. "Oh, boy, you are a comic."

Caleb's head was pulsing. Derrick's attitude made him furious. He thought Joe's son had been teasing him all night, hinting at a slim chance. Caleb knew now he would never have him.

All night he had been strangely aroused. Watching Derrick with Sophia, he had orgasmed without touching himself. Then when she reached to touch him, he couldn't let pass the chance to join in an orgy with Joe's flesh and blood. So he put his penis where Derrick's had just been and mixed his come with Derrick's on the young girl's stomach.

But he hated fucking girls. It made him feel like a soulless puppet. Still, Derrick's challenge, the scent of his sperm still hot in the air, was irresistible. Now he felt unnatural and deceived. He had tried to be friendly, for Joe's sake, Caleb told himself. And there was the hope that he could seduce Derrick, get back at Joe by turning his son queer. But the relentless sniping and straight-boy arrogance — the dismissal of any chance that a queer could hurt him. In his mind Caleb entered a furious white haze — a place where all he could do was watch himself act. He moved flesh-close to Derrick.

"Your father loves me more than you *because I'm white.*"

"What?"

Seconds later Caleb wanted to take back his words. He turned away to hide the vicious yet fearful smile he couldn't keep from his face. The boys walked silently for a moment. Derrick dropped behind a step.

Caleb felt the dull hard tips of fingers stabbing into his back. He was falling, his head snapping to the side to dodge black spokes on the wrought-iron stoop railing. His feet danced to catch themselves. As his leg slammed between two rails, his thumb was torn on a dirty shred of metal twisted away from a garbage can. Caleb turned around, putting his thumb in his mouth to suck the fine, salty stream of blood. *Finally,* he thought as Derrick shouted at him.

"My father don't need no gold-diggin' white bitch in his life. I'm putting an end to your love affair, you Caucasian homo."

A howling relish swept up from Caleb's stomach into his throat. *Finally,* he felt.

"Fuck you, Derrick!" he howled.

"Fuck you, homo."

"Your own father is a homo. You come from a homo. What does that make you?"

"You gold-diggin' white faggot Caucasian prostitute bitch."

"Your mother is a gold digger. Joseph *never* loved her. She forced herself on a gay man and made you by *mistake.*"

"He's *my* father."

"You shouldn't even *exist!*"

"Why you got to try to steal my father, huh? Huh, white pussy faggot? You think I don't know. 'Cause your own father *hates* you! I bet your father throws up just thinking about you. You know it's the truth."

Caleb stared for a moment wide-eyed. Feeling a decade of machete slashes through his heart, he flung himself at the powerful black boy, first slapping and shoving, then spitting and punching at a dark, tangible cloud. And Derrick, his mind swimming in an old pool of stillborn hate, grabbed in the storm of flailing knuckles for a thin arm he could catch and break, a finger he could quickly snap.

They fell into garbage cans, rolled perilously along the spiked iron railing, both boys getting poked in the small of the back, and then fell like dance partners onto the ground. Eggshells cracked beneath them. Sopping tea bags, a can of dried tomato paste. Caleb realized that Derrick wasn't trying to hit him anymore but only blocking his blows, holding him away. As he kicked and punched, a milk carton dripping sour milk fell over next to his head. The odor was keen and rose high in his brain like the scent of semen. Derrick's body was hard and warm, and Caleb was tired, and Derrick was just too strong.

Both of them stopped when they heard Toast call out.

"Yo, man. Jump Street!"

Toast turned and disappeared into the dark as the police car turned on its flashing lights. Derrick and Caleb stood up and started running. Ahead of them, under the light from a street-lamp, they saw Toast sprinting long-legged across the avenue.

They turned a corner and kept running. Behind them, coming fast, were short, incoherent blips of high-pitched sound. They turned another corner, and Caleb stopped suddenly.

"Get rid of the coke!" he said.

"What?" said Derrick.

"In your cuffs. Throw away the coke. They'll put you in jail if they find it."

Derrick reached into his pant cuffs and flung the packet of cocaine across the avenue.

"We didn't do anything," said Caleb. "Let's wait."

Derrick nodded. They stood with their backs against the glass storefront of a shoe-repair shop. Caleb put his hands high in the air.

"Put up your hands," he said. "Don't get nervous."

Derrick glanced over his shoulder into the storefront window. There was just a single pair of women's high-heeled shoes, on sale. Otherwise, the shop looked empty. He turned back and tentatively raised his hands halfway up. The siren became painfully loud as the blue-and-white swung around the corner and slid up onto the curb in front of them. Two officers, both white, got out of the car.

"That's right. Just stand there quiet with your hands up, and don't move," said one officer, taller than the other, with a mustache.

"Where's the other guy?" the second officer asked.

"Why did you run?" asked the taller cop.

"We were just scared," offered Derrick.

"What happened to the third guy?"

"He kept running. We saw him run straight across the avenue."

"We don't know him. We met him at the disco. He tried to sell us some drugs, but we didn't want any," said Derrick.

"You know anything about those two guys who got shot last night?"

"No, sir," said Derrick.

"We don't know nothing," said Caleb. "We heard about it, that's all."

"Why were you two fighting?"

"It was just personal, that's all. He said something about my father."

"He was trying to mug me," said Caleb in a quietly screaming voice.

"What?" asked the taller cop.

"He's lying," shouted Derrick. "He's a faggot. He wanted to suck my dick."

"Calm down. Calm down," said the shorter cop.

"God, you fucking liar," said Derrick.

"You did it to me," hissed Caleb.

"Shut your fucking mouths," shouted the shorter officer, pointing at both boys.

"You can call my father," shouted Derrick. "His name is Joseph Grant."

"I think we got a couple of homos here," said the taller cop. "We got us a *faggot* situation."

Derrick glowered with wariness at the taller cop. He felt vitally alive. His insides might have been a pinball machine, with ricocheting emotions and sensitive spots. All ringing bells and flashing lights. He remembered the Spanish boy, shot for no reason in front of his mother. What had Toast said? *Rodney King ain't had no gun.* Derrick felt a shock of fear. He didn't know that the fear in his eyes registered as a challenge to the taller policeman.

"Look at this muscle-bound buck. Make a good field slave, huh? You like white pussy, boy? You want to fuck my wife?"

"Why you got to say that?" said Derrick.

The cop glanced up at the dark sky. "Oh, thank you, God. A smart aleck. You don't say fucking shit to me, you hear me, Midnight?" The officer stepped back and pulled out his revolver.

"What are you doing, Rollie. Put the gun away." The shorter cop touched the taller one lightly on the arm, and he holstered his revolver.

"You know the law on deadly force?" said Derrick. His mind was racing, and he wasn't able to keep quiet.

"What, you got a brain, Midnight? You got a mouth?" The cop pressed his thumb into Derrick's neck. Derrick clenched his fists. The taller cop shoved Derrick back into the plate glass.

"Keep your mouth shut, Derrick!" cried Caleb.

"You started it!" Derrick's voice was hysterical. His eyes looked confused.

"You better listen to your girlfriend here, Roscoe."

The other officer stepped in between them. "Okay, okay. I get it. I seen enough." He gave the taller officer a shove backward. "Both of you assholes get in the car." He stepped to the cruiser and opened the back door. "And keep your fucking mouths shut."

"Yeah, and don't you start having sex in there either, homos." The taller cop was laughing in a booming, nervous voice. "Christ! Two fags. What next?"

New York at dawn has a precise and moving spirit. The air near its rivers carries the ancient scent of life-giving tides. Its old buildings and bridges, palpably steeped in history, silently tell stories that feel like gray memories, stripped of the who and precisely when but keeping all their meaning. And if wine becomes divine with time, so too does the musk of river water, soaked for human lifetimes into the crumbling wood of the city's failing docks. There is the knowledge of death in the river air — people have died in the night; others have barely survived — and the promise of the new day is oppressive.

Joseph was saddened as he drove over the Brooklyn Bridge, listening to Caleb's fitful explanations of the night just passed. He could barely hear the boy's high-pitched squawking; in his thoughts he was replaying the juvenile squabbling between Caleb and Derrick that had started in the lobby of the police precinct and hadn't stopped all the way along the river, through the empty midtown streets to Joseph's apartment. He had driven Derrick home first and seen him to bed. He wanted to talk to Caleb alone about a decision he had made, one that had him now near crying.

"Caleb, did you really say those things to Derrick?"

"I didn't mean it, Joe. He was really mean to me."

"I don't know what I can do now."

"I said I didn't *mean* it."

"It doesn't matter whether you meant it. You said it. How do I know what you meant? You lie all the time. You don't listen. You steal money from me. I don't know what's going on."

Caleb began chattering again, now in a more inviting voice, trying to escape through humor. "Come on, Joe. You know me. We go way back." In the past hour the boy had run a gamut of emotions — bitterness, madness, sadness, jealousy, confusion, compassion, aggression, and love — and each of them had touched Joseph. Joseph knew he would cry when he was finally alone this morning. He wouldn't drive straight home. He would come back to the bridge, watch the sun complete its morning journey, and cry.

He had never loved either of his boys so much as this morning, listening as they fought like chickens over scarce feed. Derrick was in the front of the car, Caleb jumping about in the back, then stretched out across the seat, then up with his elbows on Derrick's headrest. In the night they had become brothers, and their taunting and pecking reminded Joseph of battles with his own brother a half life ago. Wrenching memories, one more reason Joseph knew he was going to cry.

"Your son is an asshole, Joe," Caleb had said as Derrick pushed away his elbows from the headrest.

"You lucky I didn't break your neck on that street."

245

"Oh, keep wishin'."

"If my father wasn't here, I'd be beatin' your head in right now."

"Kiss my butt, Chiller."

"Dad, he told the cops I tried to mug him."

Joseph froze. There was a startling silence in the car.

"So? You told those Chinese guys I was gay."

"You are gay!"

"You set me up."

"And Dad, he says you love him more than me because he has blond hair."

"I didn't say anything about blond hair!"

"You said 'cuz you were white."

Joseph's shoulders tensed.

"Oh, kiss off," said Caleb. "You believe everything people tell you?"

"Stop the car, Dad. I'm going to throw him in the river."

"You're lucky those cops came. I was going to kick your butt."

"Those cops were real bad, Dad."

"Yeah, they called me a faggot."

"And they called me Midnight."

"Those cops hate everybody, man. Everybody that's different."

"Malcolm X was right."

"One of them asked Derrick if he wanted to have sex with his wife."

"Man, I wouldn't go near a woman crazy enough to marry that guy."

"The short one was cool."

"No, he was not cool. He was just better than the other one."

"Yeah, that tall one was a jerk."

"He pulled his gun on me. But then he put it right back because there were witnesses."

"What?" exclaimed Joseph.

"Yeah, he would have had to kill us both."

"That pig wanted to commit *murder,*" shouted Derrick.

"I wonder what happened to Toast."

"Yeah, Toast lit out, man. He was *gittin'* up."

"He broke the sound barrier, boy," said Caleb.

And then the two boys faced each other and slapped their palms. They were laughing like brothers, cursing each other like brothers, hating and loving each other like brothers.

And Joseph was hurt to remember this now — that in the night, without him, the boys had come to love each other. He'd been wrong all along to keep them apart. It was clear now that that had never been possible. They were both too strong for that. Still, he had decided, with the cold will of a hanging judge, it couldn't go on. The dawn clouds had turned rosy in the sun's orange rays. They seemed to waltz with the swaying cables of the shining old bridge. Joseph rested his hand on Caleb's thigh.

"Caleb, I don't think we can be together anymore."

Caleb was silent a long time. He put both feet up on the dashboard and sunk deep into the bucket seat. "Because of what I said to Chill?"

247

"*And* what happened with the cops. You kids! You have no idea how dangerous that was. And both of you laughing about it—"

"But you don't understand, Joe."

"No, *you* don't understand. You put my son's life in danger. I love Derrick."

"And I'm not even a glass of piss to my father, huh? Is that what you're saying?"

"Your father is very wrong. And I know you better than he does."

"Your son hates you. You should have heard what he said about gays."

"Please, just be quiet now."

"Fuck you. I'm not surprised. You were just using me for sex anyway."

"That's not true."

"Yes, it is. You used me like you used Macon. Then you left him by the river to die when you got bored."

Joseph flushed with bitter surprise and bad memory. "Stop it."

"It's true. You like to fuck young white guys up the ass, and then you dump them if they're not absolutely perfect. That's your whole life story." He kicked the dashboard with his foot. "You and Chill are ganging up on me."

Caleb cursed under his breath as they drove through downtown Brooklyn. There were the first signs of business now, people hurrying to the subway, stores unlocking their gates, street vendors selling coffee. Caleb's voice squeaked with bitterness; his curses became evil and crazy.

"This is what I get for hanging around with black people. Mr. Iazetta was right." He looked ill, almost tubercular as his skin lost its color and his face became drawn. Joseph felt again the hurt he had sensed a year ago, the powerless, rust-edged rage that had attracted him from the start.

"So that's it, huh?" Caleb peeped.

Joseph thought it better not to speak.

Caleb pounded his fist on the window. "I'm seeing another man, Joe. He's Italian. He told me not to sleep with black people. I'm going over to his house right now and have *sex*."

Joseph let Caleb out on the lawn of his father's house.

"What about work?" asked Caleb.

"You're not fired, if that's what you mean."

"Fuck you, Joe. I quit!" Caleb ran up the porch, tripping over the top step, and disappeared behind a screen door.

It was a short drive to the waterfront. Joseph felt relieved that at last he could release himself. Tears clung to his eyelashes, forming a blinding silver web when he blinked. He couldn't hold on. Coughing and trembling, he pulled over behind a grocery truck and burst into sobs.

What are you doing? he thought to himself. He started the car again. A taxi pulled out in front of him and blocked his way into the street. Joseph pounded on his car horn. "Get out of the way, get out of the way," he shouted. He pulled out across the lane and passed the taxi, then drove the several blocks back to Caleb's house.

The kid was there, sitting on the porch with his fist on his cheek, looking at a squirrel up in a tree.

PROMISE

There are too many boys like Macon Summerscale. Gay boys with bad drug habits, some of whom can't even read. Drug-raw children, and if they ever make it from Weehawken Street to the breezy dunes on Fire Island, it's only for a summer or so. One summer of money, sex, and friendship. Then their hormones get to work, squaring their jaws and swelling their hips until they're not the rare kid *in the life* anymore. To preserve the illusion of youth, they scrape their faces red with rusty razors. Smoking ketamine helps — it sinks the chest and vaporizes muscle. Boyish androgyny was the thing paid for on the chicken strolls by men who didn't care to know the difference between a woman and a man.

Wretchedness and desperation — distant cousins of innocence — are selling points on the strolls, worth a few extra dollars in the waning days of childhood. Pathos is nearly as precious as beauty in the bedrooms of gay summer beach homes. Back in the deadly city, it's the only thing a not-so-young hustler has left to sell.

This was the state that Macon was in when Joe Grant found him in Peter Rabbit's. So low, his lowliness made him proud. Willing and cheap. Stale pubic hair, dry flakes of flesh under dirty foreskins? The taste of urine? It didn't matter. He did what he had to. Sometimes for as little as a food stamp.

When Macon was twelve, his father in a gin-fired rage killed his mother with a single punch to the head. "Delirium tremens!" the old drunk pleaded in court, his rummy tears staining the Oxford Bible. Barely escaping lethal injection, instead he received fifteen to life on a work farm; Macon spent the next three years in a Catholic home for boys. In the home Macon learned the value of his knees. If he got down on them, people would keep him around a while — another summer, another day. Maybe.

One night a nun discovered him on his knees sharing his young mouth with the janitor. In the pitch-dark broom closet, the smell of bleach had clogged his nose, he couldn't breathe, and when he gagged and coughed, the Sister Superior investigated. The nuns blamed Macon — they flapped their habits and cut him in half with their stares — leaving the astonished child utterly confounded by the world around him.

Macon ran away from the home. He ran to the railroad tracks, then to men in station wagons beckoning with their index fingers or eagerly stumbling toward him over the rails as they looked this way and that for bystanders. With scars on his knees where he knelt in gravel, choking on the coal dust that flavored the air down in the rail pits, Macon learned the survival benefits of having no pride.

One man had train tickets to New York City in his brief-case. He was going to visit his wife and kid; he had missed the 4:14. Macon did him special, and while the man caught his breath and held his heart, he grabbed the briefcase and ran. There was money, a letter from the man's twelve-year-old son (*Fuck 'em,* Macon thought), and a round-tripper on the Metroliner. Macon cocked his head, remembering something about black slaves running north. In history class in the boys home, the yearlong haze of boredom had cleared for an instant — the Sister had said something about a passion for freedom that caught Macon's nebulous attention.

"I'll visit my own wife and kids," he said to himself, not knowing what he meant by this.

He spent the next summer wandering nude in the Fire Island Pines. Behind the dunes, under sensual, naked sun-sets, Macon discovered that he was beautiful. The janitor at the Catholic home never told him that, nor had the older boys taking turns in the same dark closet. And neither had the men by the railroad tracks. But in New York, for the first time ever he received affectionate praise. Something about his dark curly hair and eyes like a wolf cub's through a rifle sight.

He spent the winter in Los Angeles, modeling for a bathing suit designer. In Venice Beach he made a movie, suggesting the title himself — *Bikini Wax*. "What eyes!" the cameraman screamed, zooming in as the surf idol's come dripped off Macon's eyelash. "You make me want to give to charity!"

The following summer Macon lived in Provincetown, in a hotel suite where a palace guard of longhaired angels paraded to and from the pool in bath towels and shower clogs.

The white slavers in Provincetown had learned through experience that drugs were far more powerful than money, that with them they could make the palace guard of abandoned gay boys do anything. Macon's owner understood this especially — the boys called him Sky Daddy, for he kept them as high as the sky. Sky Daddy set cocaine out in candy dishes with carousel-colored paper straws and shiny mirror squares on lampstands, bookcases, and coffee tables.

And so the coke began to flow like sugar and oxygen in Macon's veins. If he hadn't been so accustomed to pain, he might have stopped when his nose began to sting all day and night. Each sniff was like a jet of flame squeezing up his sinus, Macon thought, but so what? Hadn't his daddy stuck his fingers in the toaster oven when he was ten? Or was that just a dream?

For Macon the experience of the drug was one of levitation, frantic horniness, and an exploding heart. There were detectives out on the window ledge, he knew. Voices from the basement sounded in the sink pipes. Macon got angry at the sun for rising. He wanted every night to last forever.

Red-eyed and witless, perpetually dizzy and high, he forgot to shave, and one day Sky Daddy caught him with a scraggly beard. Sky Daddy hated facial hair — he simply could not bear the natural course of life. In a week Macon was gone, replaced by a boy from Iowa with hairless cheeks. After kissing, one by one, good-bye to the palace guard, Macon hitched a ride from Provincetown to Boston, then took the bus to New York, where the autumn was already turning cold.

It was raining when he arrived in New York on a deathly, dreary Monday. From the bus station he went to the movies, sat up all night in a doughnut shop. In the morning his instincts led him to the front door of a transient hotel near Times Square. A white-bearded man walking a little dog came around the corner in moments, looked him up and down, and invited him up to his room for twenty dollars.

"Back in the life," he shrugged as he followed the old man up the stairs.

On the waterfront the price of sex had dropped since Macon had left for P-Town, while the price of good white powder was soaring. Squeeze, squeeze! It took Macon a day to try crack instead. He met a tall black boy named Sammy who lived with his family and was hustling to buy himself a van. In exchange for a hit, Macon gave Sammy head in the backseat. He got fucked for another, and he licked the shit off Sammy's cock for a third. When they ran out of vials, Sammy gave Macon ten dollars and sent him under the bridge to find his dealer.

"How will I know him?" Macon drawled. His accent delighted Sammy, whose penis lifted at the pathetic, lyrical sound.

"He's big." Sammy flexed both his biceps. "Hurry up back!"

And across the highway Macon ran, the stink of his own shit on his breath, then down under the bridge, to fall instantly in love with the honey-colored skin, the adamantine malice, and the bountiful drug supply of the yellow-eyed bodybuilder whom the boys on the edge of the city had nicknamed Crackman.

At this time in his life, Joe Grant was spending restless nights in the East Village. Movie night at Wonderbar, drag night at the Pyramid Club or at the Nuyorican Poets' Cafe or on the West Side at Crisco's Disco. It was in Crisco's that he met Sammy. He bought him a drink, then asked him to dance, but Sammy asked Joseph to take a walk instead — the noise in the club was annoying him. Crisco's was half a block from the river.

Dodging cars and vans, they crossed the highway and walked out onto a long, crumbling pier. For a while they stood, inches from the charred and splintered edge, watching the gulping Hudson, which looked as thick and black as oil under the blue-white moon. Joseph pulled down Sammy's zipper and rubbed him until he came. He reached for Sammy's ass. "No. Maybe later," the boy whispered.

They walked a long stretch of the riverfront, and Joseph began to get nervous. For Sammy used expressions that his son Derrick also used all the time. "Whazzup?" he called as

258

a friend flashed by on a bicycle. "I'mah jack you up, homey," he said to two Spanish kids who saw him with Joseph and laughed. "Jive-ass cracker," he yelled as a white man hollered "Faggot!" from a passing car.

In the light of the moon, Sammy's skin turned iridescent at the edges. His black skin sucked up the blackness of the night until he shone black. Blue glow about the edges, his silhouette seemed to Joseph like a man-shaped portal into happiness. He looked mortally familiar. His hair, his flowing lips, the toughness of his nose. In the salty darkness Joseph's mind began to swirl. He suffered a painful confusion, and then some inner silent mechanism took over.

"I have to go," said Joseph.

"Don't."

"I really have to."

"Can I come with you?"

Half of Joseph's nerve ends panicked and fainted. The other half all cried yes at once. He stuttered a feeble no.

Sammy pointed across the highway to a flashing neon sign that spelled out Peter Rabbit's. The sign hung above the door of a bar that opened to the street corner, right off of the highway.

"If you ever want to find me," said Sammy, "I'm in there all the time."

Sammy turned and ran away to catch his friend on the bicycle. Joseph watched him skip first and then stride away into the dark. For a flaming instant he longed to have him back. Then he rushed away in a light-headed panic, his penis inflated and livid, his tongue and throat still begging. A car almost hit him as he crossed the highway.

In eight months on the piers, Macon had never seen Crackman kill anybody. But he knew his lover meant what he said. "Do it again, you dead. Simple as that." Macon's ears were still ringing from the slap across his cheek, so he had trouble hearing what Crackman was saying. But Crackman — Dennis — had a habit of repeating things over and over, so he waited.

"Touch my product again, you dead, Macon. I'mah put one of *these* in yo skull." The giant crack dealer spoke casually as he held a .22-caliber shell between his fingertips, inspecting it in the kitchen light like a gem. The dizziness passed, and Macon stood up.

He doesn't understand, he thought. And if Crackman thought death threats would make any difference, he truly didn't understand.

But he did mean what he said. Sammy had told Macon about the drug debtors and fools who tried to cheat him whom Crackman had murdered. And the Spanish boys under the bridge still talked in sad tones about Guillermo, whom Crackman had held under water by the neck until his arms and legs stopped kicking.

Macon pulled off his pants and walked into the kitchen. Crackman huffed. "You heard me, doll baby?" Macon rubbed his lover's shoulders. Then he came around front and suckled his nipples. Crackman bent him over the oven and fucked him until the pot lids flipped over on their tops. "You mine, baby," whispered Crackman. "Baby, baby."

After, Macon stumbled into the bathroom and looked down at his stomach. An oven knob had impressed its setting bas-relief into his skin, an inch to the left of his navel.

The police in Greenwich Village knew all about Crackman and hated him. It was rumored he had killed an undercover years ago. In July the police arrested him and put him "through the system" for possession of a gram of Special K.

These were irksome days for Macon. He missed his lover's potato-shaped cock, and business by the waterfront was worse than ever. The police had hauled cement pilings in front of the highway exit where he worked, to block off traffic from the hustling trade. Macon sat on the pilings, bored and broke, wishing Sammy would show up. Sammy always talked to him, got him high, and fucked him sweeter than Crackman. But Sammy hadn't been to the river in a week. And with his lover in jail, he couldn't even get a free smoke at home. Macon cut his thumb on a curved nail jutting out of the piling. The night was dead. There wasn't a trick in sight. He gave up on the evening and walked tiredly home.

In the boardinghouse where Crackman lived, he sat down in the hallway, leaning his head against the door to their apartment. A brown mouse squeezed out from under a squeaking radiator, hurried down the hallway, and slipped under the broom-closet door.

A fantasy began to form in Macon's foggy brain, one worthy of pure peyote for all of its logic. But the beauty and excitement it produced made up for that. He could sell Crackman's stash to his ex-sky daddy for twice — no, *three times* — the price Crackman got on the street. Dennis would be so surprised when he got home from jail. Then Macon and his lover would become partners and move into one of the luxury floor-throughs that looked out over the Hudson River. There he could watch the chump two-bit hustlers sucking cock for peanuts on the piers through a telescope and laugh at them. What a beautiful idea! If only he had someone to tell about his good fortune.

"Well, since I'm gonna make him rich, Dennis won't mind if I do a little bit now." And he stood up, unlocked the door, and went inside.

He never had gotten the hang of cooking freebase; Crackman did all the kitchen work. How much water went into the pot? Not so much, apparently. And how was he supposed to know, with his ravaged sinus and spotted memory, the difference between the pink tin of pancake flour and the green one of bicarbonate of soda that Crackman expertly used to prepare his product by the pound? "Hot damn, this is complicated," Macon drawled studiously. He wasted six grams before he had a spoonful to smoke.

Then he slept for over a day. Or rather than slept, he lay down in the bed and barely budged under the sheets, holding his swollen liver all the while.

When he did get up, some thirty hours later, he telephoned Sky Daddy's New York number. "He's going to take me back for this much blow," Macon imagined as he dialed. There was no answer. He looked out the window, felt the heat, and remembered it was summer. "What was his number in Provincetown again?" He realized he hadn't ever known.

"If I go up to 52nd Street, somebody there will know him. I'll slip the doorman at Townhouse a gram and make some contacts. I'll cut a deal." This was all logical to Macon. He was certain his plan would work out, and so he went to the waterfront looking for Sammy. With his hustling business bad and his lover gone, he hadn't had sex in days, and he wanted company.

Sammy wasn't on the river, but Macon found Sammy's Jamaican friend Rags, a Spanish boy named Tito, and a white boy with a long cock named Matt and brought them all back to Crackman's hotel for a party. Rags offered to take charge in the kitchen. Macon brought him a bag of cocaine the size of a loaf of bread and told him, "Cook enough for six."

Macon opened the convertible sofa, and all four boys undressed. Finger to finger, they passed around the hot glass pipe and fucked until 5 in the morning. The coke kept his guests relentlessly erect, and Macon felt dazed and stupidly satisfied after taking turns with all three boys, especially Matt, with whom he fell in puppy love, and Tito, whom he knew from Provincetown.

By sunrise Macon's brain had turned into quicksand. His eyelids heavy as glaciers, he staggered into the bathroom and sat on the toilet, shitting loose stool and blood and holding his aching head until he fell asleep.

He hurt his neck when he snapped awake, hours, maybe a day later. He jumped up and ran into the living room. Matt, Rags, and Tito were gone. Somehow the front door had been locked. Macon sat down on the couch and started to patter on his bare knees. All of Crackman's coke was gone and probably his marijuana too. And the ketamine. He knew without looking.

Maybe not, he dreamed. Had he hidden it and forgotten? He looked in the closet, searched manically under the convertible bed, threw pillows and cushions on the floor, pulled socks and towels out of the bureau, shoved stew cans out of the kitchen cabinets down into the sink.

"Oh, God. I'm dead." Macon sighed, almost with relief. He looked down into the kitchen sink. "I'm dead as that cockroach floating in that goddamn coffee cup."

Though they had been together only for moments, Joe Grant had not forgotten Sammy. The youth's body had a potent taste, blended essence of sugar and mint, a basted Cajun flavor that Joseph could still savor weeks later by just inhaling. The memory of Sammy, the river breeze blowing across his neck, and the disturbed cry of seagulls, perhaps in answer to Sammy's unchecked night holler of ecstasy, all came back as Joseph drove along the highway. He felt a vaporous rising sensation behind his eyelids.

Peter Rabbit's, he recalled. He had walked past the famous waterfront disco many times in the past, stopped to listen to the delicious funk-rock music coming from inside. In a lusty impulse he pulled off the highway at 14th Street. He parked on a side street and briskly walked the short distance to the bar, spurred by the unlikely hope that Sammy would be there even in the early afternoon.

There were two levels inside the discotheque; the stairs to the lower level were roped off now. The long, glass-topped bar was L-shaped; on one end a set of wooden stools rested upside down, and a brass rail came to a sharp point at the corner. The curtains to the bar's storefront window were half drawn, allowing daylight in through the many spaces where black paint had chipped off, so that blotches of sun created in the room a calming, angular mix of light and shadows. At the bar, a black woman and two heavyset black men were talking. A white youth dressed in denim and corduroy leaned over the jukebox in the corner. There was no one behind the bar, and Joseph thought the place might not be open.

"Any chance of getting a drink?" he asked.

The woman turned quickly to notice him. Joseph saw that her Adam's apple protruded like a knot on a tree and thus that she was not a woman but a man. "Hello, lover," she said.

"I guess you're not really open," said Joseph.

"Oh, the bartender is taking a shit. He'll be back. Have a seat, darling." Her voice was hoarse and confident.

Joseph sat down at the short end of the L, around the corner and away from the other patrons.

"What's your name, lover?" the woman-man asked.

Joseph gestured to himself as if unsure whom she was addressing. He didn't want to talk, for the man-woman frightened him, with her slick, rising hive of hair, her neon makeup, and the night echoes in her voice. "Afternoon. I'm Joseph," he offered politely.

"Good afternoon, Joseph," she said, mocking his good manners. "My name is Miss Moneypussy."

Joseph chuckled with surprise. The man-woman pointed to the two men beside her.

"This is Fat Blackie, and *that*" — she grunted — "is Bonehead Ben." She gestured over her shoulder with a green-painted fingernail. "And over there trying to jimmy the juke-box is Miss White Trash of 1995, Macon Summerscale!"

"You better stop calling me that," said the man referred to as Bonehead.

"Pay no attention to him, Joseph. He's a little slow." Her voice sounded like a snore, like a foghorn.

"Give me some pussy, you ho. That's all you good for."

"Bonehead Ben, if you were Swami Kashoggi's sole heir, you still could not afford this *twat*!" Her eyes turned chilly. "You mutant piece of frog turd."

Just then the bartender appeared from behind a swinging door.

The boy in denim had heard his name and turned around. His eyes fixed keenly on Joseph, and he walked directly to the corner of the bar. First he rested his elbows on the rail and glanced at Miss Moneypussy. Then he looked again at Joseph and held out his hand.

"What's up, bro'?" he said in a low voice.

Joseph shook the outstretched hand, which was dirty and cold. Desire registered immediately, and he stared unsubtly, sizing up the kid.

His boots were too big. His shoulders were raised in a posture of stress. He was dirty. And his voice couldn't really be so deep. *Bad news,* thought Joseph. But the boy's body seemed to flow from top to bottom like cream, in a way that made the blood bubble in Joseph's penis.

"My name is Macon," he said in a voice more likely his own. "You know what they say? 'Macon's got the bacon.' " He tugged at his crotch. His light Southern accent sounded like sweet singing to Joseph.

"I like how you talk," Joseph said.

Macon grinned painfully. "I come from *way* down South. Atlanta, Georgia." Joseph placed the accent as farther north, Virginia or Maryland, perhaps.

More lies began to flow readily. "Yep, my family has lived in Georgia for centuries. We owned slaves, I'm sad to say, but we set them all free. My granddaddy was in the Klan. I'm ashamed of that."

Joseph looked for relief at the bar. Miss Moneypussy made a face.

"Yep, I seen Hank Aaron hit the big one."

Joseph cleared his throat.

"My father owns a chain of seafood restaurants in Georgia. He wants me to manage the business but, you know, got to run wild." He did a little two-step and circled his hands.

267

"*Getcha motor runnin'*. Sow mah wild oats. I come North. Boston, Philly."

Joseph grew impatient. A car pulled up in front of the bar, and the boy vanished into the ladies' room.

Miss Moneypussy gestured confidentially to Joseph. "That stupid-ass child is in so much trouble. Got no place to live, but that won't be a problem for long."

"Hah!" interrupted Ben, hovering over her shoulder. She moved closer to Joseph.

"Crackman looking for his idiotic ass. He *will* be dead quite shortly. I'd bet my Japanese silk brassiere, by midnight tomorrow, Miss White Trash of 1995's beauty reign," she paused, "will terminate quite abruptly."

After a short while, Macon peeked and then came out of the ladies' room. Fat Blackie hollered to him, "Hey, Macon, you seen Crackman lately? I got to talk to him."

"That's real fuckin' funny, Fat Blackie."

"Well, you tell him when you see him I want to buy some crack. On spec. My credit is good." And Fat Blackie hooted a laugh of death, sweet with the arrogance that the living save for the soon-dead. Macon's face sunk, and he walked back over to the jukebox. Joseph asked the bartender for a drink and followed him.

"What are they talking about?" he asked.

"Nothin'. I got in a little trouble. I need to get out of town." Macon nervously ran his fingers across the buttons on the jukebox. "Where do you come from, New Jersey?" he stuttered.

Joseph grew bold, sensing the boy's terror. "Do you know a boy named Sammy? A tall black kid?"

"Oh, God, Sammy? Hell, yeah, I know him. He's my lover."

"He told me he comes in here."

"Oh, yeah?" Macon hesitated. "Listen, bro', if you looking for some nut, how about me?" He came close and breathed hot drops of spit into Joseph's ear. "I do anything for not too much money." He paused and came close again. "I really need a train ticket."

Joseph could smell the helplessness. It roused him so that he felt faint.

"I'll hook you up with Sammy too. We could do a trio." The drawl now was palpable, a slow, warm breath that seemed to blow all the way from Virginia. "You could watch him fuck me."

Joseph's penis felt like a weight in his pocket. Part of him wanted to kill the desperate slut.

"Forty dollars," said Macon.

"No thank you," said Joseph. He was an indecisive predator. His eyes fell on the boy's daisy-petal mustache. Then on his smudged hands. The erotic opportunity! This dirty Southern urchin, lovely as a bowl of cream, flicking a tiny red tongue, was begging for his life.

"Okay. If you need a place to hide."

In Joseph's apartment they sipped wine and talked about their lives until late in the evening. Macon picked up the phone at midnight and called for take-out pasta; when he hung up he smiled at Joseph as if he had mastered a task. Slowly the fear drained out of Macon — it seemed he was thawing. He moved his arms and legs more casually now. Occasionally he ticked his head to shake his hair from his eyes. At the bar his neck had been rigid, his hair hanging dumbly in his face.

It was around 2 o'clock. Joseph sat in a wooden chair, in a red T-shirt, naked from the waist down. Macon was in just his crusty corduroys, on his knees, pleasing him with his tongue and tender throat. It was understood, if Macon was good Joseph would keep him. In a mirror Joseph watched the mop of brown hair bob and dip. Lovely rhythm. He gushed and bit his lip. Oh, the distilled melancholy of such desperate supplication! He tipped the boy's head back with his fingers and came on his chin with a radiance he had never known.

They stayed in together for several days. Joseph worked at home because he didn't trust Macon alone in his apartment, and he didn't yet want the boy to leave — he wanted to invest some of his life in this curious, dangerous situation.

After two days Macon telephoned Sammy, who told him that Crackman was asking around, that he still wanted to kill him but didn't know where Macon was. Sammy came over that evening, and Joseph watched the two boys make love. As Sammy and Macon kidded and laughed, he felt like a camp counselor, a school crossing guard, a mother. He offered to cook dinner for them, sent Sammy to the store for steaks and a bottle of gin. The two boys got drunk and fell asleep. While they slept, Joseph watched them, jealous of them both, for he loved them both, and it was clear that they loved each other.

After three nights and days of dominant sex — slapping, spanking, coming in his face — Joseph didn't touch Macon again. He felt guilty, for he wasn't sure what he would do with him. Macon couldn't stay much longer, nor did Joseph want him to, for he had taken all the pleasure he could from enslaving the child. Macon's plight no longer excited him — it saddened him and made him too sick for sex. Yet if he put him out... Perhaps he could drive him to the railroad station and give him money to leave town. Yes, that was an idea.

He stepped out of the apartment, absentmindedly, to clear his head, breathe fresh air, and make a plan. He ran to the post office and supermarket. It was risky to leave Macon alone, and so he hurried back to his apartment, having decided to pay the kid's way out of town. When he stepped off the elevator, Macon was standing in the doorway in Joseph's bathrobe, holding open the door for him.

"Sammy called." Macon's eyes were bright. "Crackman got shot last night. Rags and Tito *killed* him." And the delivered boy thrust his torso into Joseph's arms and hugged him.

Macon rushed about the apartment, putting away groceries, picking up papers and dirty clothes. He brought Joseph a glass of ice water, pulled off his shoes, offered to make him dinner. When Joseph declined, he sat in his lap and put his arm affectionately around his shoulder. "You saved me, Joe." He slid his bare rump out from the bathrobe and down between Joseph's legs. "Tonight, I want all this inside of me."

And that night in Joseph's bedroom, Macon offered up his bottom — his beauty, his worth, all that he had, he believed. And it was...oh, so beautiful. This boy had breathed death, and it had been horribly real — solid, unmoving, like wood, like iron. Macon had dreamed of the knife, felt in his nightmares the burst of brick against his skull. And he had sniffed the indignity that his death would be irrelevant, that people would laugh, Fat Blackie would tell stories. The explosion of light in his head or of fire in his stomach would matter to no one but him.

It occurred to Joseph as he unrolled a condom, then entered the shivering boy, that he had never known real fear. Not urgent terror, not as Macon had. But he could imagine the sensation. *Crackman is dead! I'm not gonna die!* Then the flight of emotion — the taking off, the bird's-eye view of time. Reprieve.

Macon fell into the blankets and cried as Joseph licked his teeth like an uncaring fox. He had saved a life, and this glowing bottom was his reward. His prize was, this once, to be a beast, to take satisfaction like a wolf. The sex quickly became vicious and sweet. Macon let him play at ripping savagery.

The bedroom faded into a blind spot; Joseph was aware only of ringing lust, of sex buzzing about like wasps. Through a light haze at his pupils, he saw the lovely Southerner flinching, his head turned flat on a pillow. The pink lips, partly open, the parted white teeth behind them. Wondrous sound washed against his ears. The room echoed with squeals and chirps and shouts of surprise. A counterpoint of oboes and flutes, occasionally a bowed cello. And high in the overtones — high, high! — infuriating strains of agony, surrender, and delight.

He crushed the boy's back against the bed board, holding the small brown head in his arms like a football. Macon did his best not to fall off the bed, to stay put and receive — so beautiful, the submission.

Later in a dream Joseph saw himself watching Macon and Sammy kissing in his bed. Joseph got into the bed, and Macon disappeared. He put his arms around Sammy instead. In the dream Joseph became fantastically, magically erect.

He woke with a violent start to find Macon fiddling with his testicles.

Two weeks later Macon showed up at the apartment at 4 in the morning wearing neither pants nor shoes. Joseph's face flashed bright with alarm, and Macon shrunk from his unbelieving glare. "Hi, Joe," he said, his face a dizzy blur; then he turned off the lamp and fell asleep on the sofa.

In the early afternoon Joseph brought him a cup of hot tea. "You can't stay here anymore," he said.

Macon looked at him passively. "Okay," he shrugged. Getting kicked out was a ritual for him, like Palm Sunday.

They shared a quiet breakfast. Joseph had nothing to say, but Macon rambled on, avoiding Joseph's eyes, his voice a

273

soothing muddle. "I really love you, Joe. You're the best man I ever knew. You saved my worthless, piece-of-shit life. I owe you."

He had turned a trick in the stairwell of the building, he admitted. The man was very strong, and when he became brutal, Macon kicked him and ran half naked up the stairs.

"My pants are probably still down there," he said, his eyes rolling with a casualness that baffled Joseph as would a Buddhist mystery.

"I'm sorry, but you still have to leave."

Joseph gave him a pair of sweatpants and some old running shoes, a windbreaker, and fifty dollars to buy new clothes. They searched the stairwell, and Macon was right. His jeans and cowboy boots were on the second floor. "The fucker stole my underpants," said Macon.

The next day Macon and Joseph drove down the highway to Greenwich Village. They didn't say very much in the car. Macon got out on Tenth Street, not at all far from Peter Rabbit's.

"Say hi to Sammy" were Joseph's last words.

"I'm sorry I messed up" were Macon's.

From time to time Macon would visit, even spend the night, have dinner and sex, or visit with Sammy, but Joseph soon grew afraid of him. While murder hung over the boy, Joseph had never truly seen him — he saw only his terror and his longing to live. Now he could see the dope rage behind his eyes, the baffling randomness of Macon's thoughts.

Macon didn't accept his banishment at first. He would wait on the corner or sit for hours on the stoop. When Joseph drove up one day, saw him on the doorstep, and without speaking drove away, Macon at last believed there was no reason to come back.

Was it the function of leaves to diffuse light? Was there form in even that? Joseph pondered the plant life in the bramble as he walked, searching for ideas for his next painting. Turning to his right, he came upon two twins, with nearly white trunks and yellow leaves, that were losing their bark. Surrounded by a gnarly brown family of very thick trunks, the twins reached to escape into the sky and thinned out tenuously. One of them was wounded; among its low branches was a sawed-off amputation.

Elsewhere in the woods were diverse little colonies — tall and short, straight and crooked, black-brown or beige or yellow or bronze — organized in exclusive clumps of sameness. Some sagged to the ground. Others bushed out into hives, short, bullish, thorny nests. Some evolved slowly up from the trunk, turning less thick, then thin, then into twigs. A few aspired skyward, to heaven. One exploded suddenly into thin, frail limbs that could barely hold up its dense cluster of leaves.

Joseph sat down on a stump and reached into his coat pocket. Somewhere in the threaded folds was a letter from Caleb that he had read twice already, and it warmed him so, opening his pores each time. Caleb was in Israel with his mother. Now, as Joseph looked for inspiration in the woods, he wanted to read it again. Or just feel it in his hands. To remember the boy, two years older now, whose pain he still felt he had exploited.

To answer your question, I don't have any plans. I'll stay here with my mom at least a year. I need to spend time here.

Yes, Joseph thought. Caleb needed a change. He had given him all he could.

But thanks anyway a lot for writing to me. It was good to hear news from New York. Especially the news about Derrick. Bet you can't wait to smell those shitty diapers, huh? Grandpa!

Joe, don't be mad at your kid for getting that girl pregnant. You and I did some crazy things in the heat of passion too. Remember?

Joseph certainly remembered.

The men in Israel are really hot. I want one of these hot commandos. Strapped, dark, sexy killers. I haven't figured out the gay scene here yet, but I will. If I meet the right man,

277

I might never come back to America.
   Love always, Caleb

Joseph held the letter to his face, imagining he could smell Caleb's scent. He folded it and put it back in his pocket. Then he closed his eyes and visualized a collage of colors — mostly yellows and greens — formal contradictions, fluidly evolving shapes. His next painting. He hurried home, holding the imagery in his mind.

More than likely it was the last snowfall that early spring. The branches of the lone tree visible from Derrick's window looked as if they had been dipped in white chocolate, coated with frost so carefully and intimately. The streetlamps were lit, though the sun hadn't yet completely set out of the sky, and so, above the buildings was still a grayish blue, but in the street it looked like night.

Derrick looked far up the street. An old man unsteadily navigated the slush, his Eskimo cap tilted on his head. In one hand he gripped a wooden cane. He looked exhausted and yet energized by the prospect of soon arriving home. From the other direction came a young man carrying a gym bag. As they passed, the distance between them rapidly expanded, the youth walking faster until he was out of sight. The old man came to his doorway. He slipped to his knees on ice, then made his way up the stoop and disappeared through the front door. A minute later a light went on behind a window shade on the first floor.

The snowfall in the street had been scattered by traffic. Along the sidewalk, though, it survived, still thick and clean. Derrick leaned out very far to see the shining white, and there he saw him. A young man in a leather jacket, leaning against the streetlamp. The sloppy way he stood looked familiar. Derrick ran to the closet, put on his hooded sweatshirt, and bounded down the stairs to the doorstep.

Once downstairs he asked the vagrant, "Yo, you waiting for somebody?" His voice was aggressive because he was cold.

The vagrant's reflexes were slow. He turned his head with seemingly great effort and stared curiously, almost impudently. "Yes, I am," he drawled. "I'll only be here a minute. You can go back inside."

"Are you waiting for a man named Joe?"

"Joe Grant. That's right." The vagrant youth nodded his head deliberately, studying Derrick's face, and in seconds he seemed to have realized something.

"It's cold out here. Come into the hall and wait," said Derrick. "He should be home from work in a little while."

Inside the lobby, Derrick stared into the young man's face, which looked weathered, thin, and old. His hair and eyebrows had snow in them. The flatness in his brown eyes stirred up sympathy in Derrick.

He knew who it was. Macon Summerscale from Baltimore. Caleb had told him how his father had saved Macon's life.

"My father might be a while," Derrick said. "Why don't you come upstairs?"

Macon stomped the wetness off of his cowboy boots. "Okay, thanks," he said.

Derrick glanced down at the brown-and-white snakeskin, more worn than he remembered, and looked up smiling. Macon cocked his head questioningly.

"This way," said Derrick. He started up the stairs.

"Can we take the elevator?" whispered Macon.

"Sure."

When Joseph arrived home, his crack addict ex-lover and his son were sitting across from each other in the living room, watching television. Macon held a cup of steaming coffee in his hands.

Derrick switched off the television as soon as his father entered the room. Surprise registered on Joseph's face as a frown, though he wasn't angry. But he seemed so to Derrick, who stood up and apologized.

"I saw him standing downstairs on the stoop, Dad. I recognized him."

"It's all right, Derrick." Joseph turned to Macon. "How are you?"

"How you doing, Joe?"

"Fine." He paused. "What are you doing here?"

"I came by 'cause I had to see you. Are you pissed?"

"I'm just really surprised."

"Do you want me to split? Can I stay a little bit? It's bitchin' cold outside."

"No, no. You can stay a little while." Joseph looked at Macon, remembering the first day he ever saw him and knowing now from hellish experience to study the texture of his skin in the semilighted room. There was an off-white growth the size of an apple seed in the corner of his right eye. And Joseph could also see that his breath was labored.

"Derrick, why don't you go for a short ride?" He tossed his son his car keys. "Just a few minutes." He handed Derrick a twenty-dollar bill. "You can bring back dinner if you want. Chinese?"

Derrick nodded.

"You want to have dinner, Macon?"

"Chinese? Wow! That sounds great."

Derrick pulled on his sneakers and overcoat and left. When the front door slammed behind him, Joseph sat across from Macon on the living-room sofa.

"How do you feel, Macon?" asked Joseph.

"Not that good, Joe. My hair..." He pulled at a few strands and then wriggled his fingers in frustration. "My hair is thinning out. Somebody told me it was psoriasis. And stuff is coming up out of my — my thing." He pointed toward his crotch. "My dick. White stuff is pouring out. I think it's gonna stop—" He took a long breath. "It's *gotta* stop soon."

"How about your throat?"

"Oh, it's, like, sore. It's sore all the goddamn time."

Joseph put his palm to his chin, nestled his cheek against his knuckles, and stared glumly at the Southern runaway he had once loved. They sat for a long moment, both in silence, as Joseph tried to block his thoughts from taking shape as words.

He took a deep sigh. "Well, listen, spend the night. Have dinner with us."

"Thanks, Joe. It's cold as fuck out there."

"I see you've been talking with Derrick. You like him?"

"Oh, he's so cool, Joe. He's hip. And he looks great. So healthy."

Joseph snickered. Macon was talking of Derrick not as a peer but as an older man would. Impressed by youth. Macon seemed, and truly was, much older than when he first met him.

"Yes. He works out all the time."

"You know who he looks like?"

Joe's eyes flared slightly. "No, who?"

"Sammy! Don't you think so?"

"Maybe a little."

"They look like twins." Macon became a bit animated, almost seeming to dance in the recliner.

"Not like twins!"

Macon hesitated. "Your son knows about you? I mean, he knows who I am?"

"It's a long story. And if I tell it to you now, I'm gonna need a quart of Tylenol."

Macon looked blankly into space with his neck stretched and his head seeming to float over his body. "It's a trip, ain't it, Joe? All this gay stuff." A death shadow fell across his eyes, and a halo of death made his head appear to glow in the

283

dim living-room light. He shook his head slowly. "It's one mean fucking bitch."

Macon stayed for the next few weeks. He and Derrick played cards, told jokes, made fun of each other, and, when they had the house alone, talked personally and privately — intensely so — about Joseph.

Derrick enjoyed the confidence and company of his house-guest, even while he laughed at Macon's flights of illogic. One afternoon he came home from college and found Macon on the telephone, deep into a conversation with Derrick's girlfriend, Wanda, who had called collect from Cincinnati. In private afterward, Derrick asked Wanda what they had talked about. She was reticent to talk about it; she said only that he had sounded very sad.

Derrick knew Macon was sick. When Macon tired in the evenings, Derrick would clear his dinner plates from the coffee table. He figured out the times when it was best not to bother him. For the first time since that autumn, in Joseph's home Macon ate and rested well. The winter drained out of his bones and lungs. And soon he seemed much better — better spirited and stronger, except for the night that his prostate swelled to the size of a cat's-eye marble.

In the middle of the evening, he suddenly began groaning. In two minutes he was screaming. Joseph and Derrick came running into the living room. Macon, his eyes wild and tearing, was squeezing his buttocks with both palms, crying like an infant one moment, then cursing venomously and horribly the next. He bounced his bottom on the sofa seat cushion, then jumped up squealing and chopping his teeth and fell to the floor on his knees.

"Ow, ooh, ow! Christ!" he hissed. "Oh, goddamn, goddamn, goddamn, goddamn. Oh, please, *God. Please.*"

Derrick watched, his eyes afire with curiosity and panic, the white boy shaking and banging his head on the floor. Joseph grabbed his son by the shoulders and led him quickly to the front door, putting his car keys in Derrick's palm.

"Go downstairs and start the car." He spoke calmly. "Wait downstairs for me, okay? He's got to go to the hospital."

The doctor punctured Macon's prostate gland with a long gold needle, and after a minute of shrieking, the pain stopped. Macon was sedated and then rolled on a sheeted gurney into the emergency room hallway. Derrick sat, saddened but with his questions grimly answered, in the waiting room while the doctor avoided telling Joseph what he hadn't doubted for three weeks.

"There are a number of indications that concern me. He's very ill. You say he has a history of drugs?"

"Yes, drugs," said Joseph. "And prostitution."

"Well, the tests will tell us more in a few hours." The physician yawned and tugged at her pockets. "The swollen glands aren't necessarily HIV, especially in a drug abuser. But there is something in the throat that, I'm sorry, is very troubling. I'm terribly sorry."

He rested in the hospital for blood tests and treatment about three days. Then Macon came back to stay with my father and me. Fine with me, I told Pop. Macon was funny in the morning when he had energy. He had this hillbilly act he was so proud of — that was his personality. He'd curse and talk like he came from Texas, which he didn't, but it made me laugh, like he was putting on a show for me. By the afternoon he got tired and started talking like an old man. I couldn't bear to listen to him then.

Once we stayed up all night, just chilling. Macon talked about his life as a prostitute. He told me how my father saved his life when this drug pusher was hunting him down to murder him, and Pop took him in off the streets until these other gay kids shot the dealer dead under the 59th Street Bridge. Then Pop kicked him out because he was too wild.

Macon said twenty years of life was a bargain, since he wasn't supposed to be born in the first place. That upset me because I wasn't supposed to be born either, my father being gay, you know. It was strange how Macon used his own father's hatred to get ready to die. "I got over on the Lord," he said, and his eyes lit up. Sometimes it seemed like Macon was proud of being near death, like it set him apart from me.

Macon said the way to handle dying was to open up your heart until rapture and love sweeps over you. "You got to catch the Holy Spirit," he told me in his phony Texas accent. He said he hoped to see his mother again, though he didn't know how all that worked.

Cool, but I was curious about my father. So Macon told me how Pop fell in love with a black kid that looked just like me and then freaked out. That was before he met Macon or Caleb. The black kid's name was Sammy Cavinaw. Macon showed me a picture. He didn't look anything like me, but Macon kept saying, "Twins, twin brothers."

So I went up to 99th Street by the East River Drive in Spanish Harlem, where Sammy played basketball on Saturday afternoons, according to Macon, to get a closer look at my so-called twin. I knew I'd recognize him from his picture. As always, I was right. I stood outside the court watching him play ball — he wasn't bad rebounding, considering he's a homo. He was tall and skinny, with bony knees and pink lips and a faggy haircut. He didn't look like me, I don't care what Macon said.

He had to notice me staring so hard. He dribbled over close to the fence, trying to see if he recognized me. Then he tried to woof me; he looked me in the eye to back me down. I

287

didn't want him thinking I was looking for sex, so I was shaky. Sammy passed the basketball back to the other cats playing and started toward me.

I walked away as fast as I could without running. When I looked back, he was still coming, onto the sidewalk now. Damn, I've never been so nervous in my life. I walked under the overpass that crossed the highway to the East River. Traffic was roaring past me. I stood there under the overpass a minute and caught my breath. Then I turned to head home, but there was Sammy still following me. Now I was mad. I was going to punch him right in his head. When he got close I looked into his eyes, fierce.

"Ain't you Derrick?" he said.

I took a step back.

"Yeah?"

"Yes," I said.

"Joe's kid? I seen pictures of you, mister."

I was flabbergasted.

"What you doing up here? Don't tell me Joe—"

"My father is fine." *Don't even mention it.*

"Cool. So why you looking for me all the way up in *El Barrio*?"

"Macon told me you play ball up here."

"Macon is still alive?"

"He's pretty sick."

"I know. You getting all into your father's business now, huh?"

I nodded.

"I still see Joe now and then."

"You and my father?"

"Yep."

"No."

"Yes, sir. Let me show you something."

I probably looked like an owl. Pop still being his sneaky self.

Sammy showed me his business card. A REAL BLACK MAN WITH A VAN, it said. "Walk with me, and I'll show you."

So we walked back around the basketball court and up the street. Sammy's van was parked on the corner. It was a little banged-up but very colorful.

"Your father and I painted it."

Yep. I recognized Pop's whacked-out painting style. Yellow loops and pink circles and black streaks. I started tripping.

"I got to book, man," and I shook Sammy's hand and left in a rush.

"Say hello to Joe," he called after me.

I never said a thing to Pop. But what a trip. Pop still getting down — and with this cool brother with the psychedelic van. My father is lucky he *is* gay. I mean, women don't go for the droopy, nervous type. I'm sorry, but Pop couldn't catch the rap with a female in a hundred years. But he knows how to rap to dudes, evidently.

Macon kept getting sicker. My father was on the telephone for days fighting with the social workers. He even called a lawyer about suing the city. He was trying to find a place for Macon to live out his life. He was yelling into that telephone, man. "You want a lawsuit? I *don't* want to hear

289

it." Damn, Pop has a big mouth. For a nerd he got evil with those social workers.

Pop went temporarily insane about this time. Talking to himself in the bathroom, cursing at the president and the damn health commissioner and the mayor. Finally they found a hospice for Macon to live in, and Pop calmed down. Macon stayed there through the summer and winter, and when we went to visit, he told me it wasn't so bad. The last time I saw him was this past spring. He died about the start of summer.

Two days after Macon died, I found a handwritten sheet of paper in my father's desk. I snoop in his business all the time — I'm like that. It was a pencil draft of his will, leaving his business and bank account to me, some to my mother. And a thousand bucks apiece to a bunch of gay stuff, Macon's hospice, and Gay Africans and Gay Health.

I don't want Pop to go like Macon did. Damn! Jumping up and down and screaming, falling down the stairs, nodding off at dinner, hair falling out. I don't know if I could take it. If he ever needs a hospice, I'll knock those social workers out if they don't get him one quick. I hope to God it doesn't happen. But if my father dies, I'll double those gifts to those AIDS places. I don't need the money.

Pop left money to my mother in trust for my baby. Yeah, I got my girlfriend pregnant. Pop was furious! Waving a box of rubbers in my face. Threatening to put me in the Army. Hollering about now he has to pay for another baby. Mistake or not, now I'm glad I did it. Wanda is too. She'll be a beautiful mother.

I've known Wanda since I was twelve. She was a little tomboy. We used to take the trolley out to the last stop in Cincinnati — me, her, and my friend Dutch — then take the ferry to the farm country. Wanda led the way as we followed dirt roads out into the tall grass and woods. In the country she acted more like a girl, fussing over sunflowers and white-yellow butterflies, pointing up at the tops of trees.

One time I had to piss bad, so I told her not to look. Her face turned devilish, and she turned back into a tomboy. "Go ahead and pee then — what you worried about?" Dutch was laughing at me dancing to keep from wetting my pants. I knew Wanda — she wasn't ever going to turn around, and I couldn't wait, so I whipped it out. As soon as the air and sun hit me, I bloomed like a flower. I stood on my toes and swung my thing in the air like a mud-red wand. And there Wanda was, fussin' over it like one of her caterpillars or yellow-leaf daisies. She touched it, then Dutch did too, and then both of them were playing with it. I kept on growing. Inside my chest I felt like a balloon that was about to burst. "Go ahead and pee," Wanda told me, so I let go, and here I came like a rainbow. Then I was down in the grass with Wanda's tongue in my mouth and her panties stuck in my hair. I was inside her, and Dutch was running his hand down my back and up and down my behind.

I couldn't sleep that night when I got home. My legs cramped up in the bed, and I kept feeling like a balloon in my chest. I was twelve. I was so young, my nerves were too sensitive — like tender, just-born plant buds. Bright green so you can smell the freshness. Do you remember?

This is how I felt when I imagined my father in bed with Caleb, all wrapped-up arms and legs in white sheets with that white boy. I felt like a kid discovering sex. Tripping, it was so new and intense. I'm a man, bro. I don't like feeling like a kid.

My mother and father were never in love like me and Wanda. All I remember is Ma shouting at Pop, calling him selfish and arguing with him on the telephone. I asked her, "Why you so rough on Pop?"

She said he needed it. "We have to be hard on your father, honey, or he'll stay a little boy all his life." And I wondered why would somebody have a kid if he was still a kid himself.

Caleb said that I shouldn't even exist, that I was an accident my father didn't want to happen. And when I realized my father never was naturally hot for my mother, that did bother me. But I don't worry about that now, since nothing Pop does makes sense anyhow. He probably might want a house to fall on his head, just to try it. If somebody offered him the keys to the castle, he'd say, "No, that's okay." My father is wack.

And I know he loves me, accident or not. He loves me like the sun shines on the moon. He loves me the way rabbits run through a forest. I'm a blessing to him. He says so all the time. And even if deep in his heart he wants to hold me like one of his boyfriends or cook for me like he was my wife — well, Pop is just wack.

We went for a walk in Central Park a few days after Macon died. We brought lunch, Pop brought a new book, and we sat out on a meadow I remembered playing on as a kid with my friend Terry.

A woman came along carrying a little kid in her arms, though he looked too big for that, about five or six. She set him down on the grass and spread out a black-and-white bath towel and then picked him up again and set him down on the towel. He had mad skinny legs, too skinny, and he just lay there on the towel like a newborn. I wondered what was up. Then I saw, his legs were useless. He couldn't walk.

His skin was very pale. He lay on his back on the towel, rolling back and forth from the waist. All he could move was his hips, not his arms or legs. But he could roll. Rolling was his way, natural as walking. He rolled like other kids run and play.

He just wouldn't stay on that towel. When his mother left him for a minute to go to the water fountain, he made his escape. He rolled off the towel onto the grass, pulling his legs around slowly like a praying mantis. Looking up over his neck, upside down, his eyes wide and hungry. I wanted to go talk to him — but it was enough just to meet his eyes and communicate that way.

His mother came back and stood over him with her hands on her hips. "Where do you think you're going?" she asked.

He was five feet from the towel by then. He would have rolled across the meadow if she hadn't come back.

Pop put his arm around my shoulder. We watched the boy's mother speak to him, and I wondered what that was like for him. Man, the world would be rough on that kid without her. I couldn't think about that. I wanted to see the positive. He was a blessing to his mother. He didn't know enough to regret anything.

Pop talked to me as we watched. He didn't look at me, he just talked.

"Derrick, I don't know what would have happened if I had still been in the closet with you when Macon showed up. I'm afraid I would have turned him away rather than let you find out I was gay."

"I think I already knew, Pop."

He smiled and went on as though he hadn't heard me.

"You saved my soul, buddy. It would have killed me to turn my back on that kid."

"I'm glad we helped him, Pop."

Just then the boy's mother picked him up and walked away into the trees.

And I felt all the world, the seas, all of time rushing inside of me.

You know, I hated Macon the first time I saw him. Some white motherfucker waiting on the stoop for my dad like it was *his* dad.

That doesn't bother me anymore. I don't know why; it just doesn't.

alyson
books

B-BOY BLUES, by James Earl Hardy. A seriously sexy, fiercely funny, black-on-black love story. A walk on the wild side turns into more than Mitchell Crawford ever expected. "A lusty, freewheeling first novel.... Hardy has the makings of a formidable talent." *–Kirkus Reviews*

2ND TIME AROUND, by James Earl Hardy. The sequel to the best-seller *B-Boy Blues.* "An upbeat tale that—while confronting issues of violence, racism, and homophobia—is romantic, absolutely sensual, and downright funny." *–Publishers Weekly*

MY BIGGEST O, edited by Jack Hart. What was the best sex you ever had? Jack Hart asked that question of hundreds of gay men, and got some fascinating answers. Here are summaries of the most intriguing of them. Together, they provide an engaging picture of the sexual tastes of gay men.

MY FIRST TIME, edited by Jack Hart. Hart has compiled a fascinating collection of true, first-person stories by men from around the country, describing their first same-sex sexual encounter.

THE DAY WE MET, edited by Jack Hart. Hart presents true stories by gay men who provide intriguing looks at the different origins of their long-term relationships. However love first arose, these stories will be sure to delight, inform, and touch you.

THE PRESIDENT'S SON, by Krandall Kraus. President Marshall's son is gay. The president, who is beginning a tough battle for reelection, knows it but can't handle it. *"The President's Son...*is a delicious, oh-so-thinly veiled tale of a political empire gone insane." *–The Washington Blade*

THE LORD WON'T MIND, by Gordon Merrick. In this first volume of the classic trilogy, Charlie and Peter forge a love that will survive World War II and Charlie's marriage to a conniving heiress. Their story is continued in *One for the Gods* and *Forth Into Light.*

HORMONE PIRATES OF XENOBIA AND **DREAM STUDS OF KAMA LOKA,** by Ernest Posey. These two science-fiction novellas have it all: pages of alien sex, erotic intrigue, the adventures of lunarian superstuds, and the lusty explorations of a graduate student who takes part in his professor's kinky dream project.

These books and other Alyson titles are available at your local bookstore.
If you can't find a book listed above or would like more information,
please call us directly at 1-800-5-ALYSON.